I0819887

GRACE FLYNN

Written and Created by:

CATHALSON

CATHAL ENTERTAINMENT

*Pursue * Life * Magically* Invent * Imagination*

PUBLISHING HIGHLY IMAGINATIVE LITERATURE - SINCE 2005

cathalson.com

GRACE FLYNN
Written by Cathalson
cathalson.com

Published by: CATHAL Entertainment

Cover by Philip Lee McCall II

Cover Art by: Terry Huddleston

ISBN-13: 9780982265635

Printed in the United States of America
1st Edition / Printed: July 2019

This book is dedicated to:
Frances & Olivia Lee McCall

THE PIRATE AND I

My adventures with Grace Flynn, began the day my daughter was born. The journey of being a father had just begun and at its start I began to examine my own life and the people, who had an impact upon it.

As I took inventory of what made me who I am, I realized that many powerful women had left their imprint upon my heart and mind. From them I had learned the strength of bravery, when the world grows dark.

I also learned from these women, that there is no greater power than love and the act of sacrifice. Lessons that would shape me forever.

It was then I looked for heroes in media, that my daughter could look up to, ones that broke stereotypical roles within our history and society…I found very few!

I then decided…that I would create a hero for my daughter and all the others who were searching for a hero…like no other.

Captain Grace Flynn was born, and quickly she began to show others just how amazing and special was. Grace became more than a just little girl's hero…she now belonged to everyone!

~CATHALSON

PRELUDE - A WOMAN IN THE DARK
MONT ORGUEIL - ISLE OF JERSEY

Darkness...A sanctuary and a living hell balanced in perfection. She discovered that it was devoid of both love and hate, while it soothed and terrified those caught within its deepest patches of shadow.

The cold and damp floor had become her constant companion for days, perhaps weeks. She was quite unsure how long it had truly been, for without the light of the sun, passage of time was indistinguishable.

She had killed a dozen rats that had wondered into her cell either scavenging for food or following the scent of her previously oozing wounds. This was something she knew and could hold on to, as the abyss of inner madness sought to cloud her mind. Each rodent had become an unwilling sacrifice in a dark ritual that helped to heal her injuries and kept her ebbing strength from leaving her body entirely.

She slowly chewed upon a cloth within her mouth, drawing out the bitter taste of blood and grime. This was her secret and her only chance for survival. It was a small square piece of a magical scarf known as the Bloodsilk. Once it had been part of a blood red flowing scarf, which had been her talisman and the reason her enemies had dubbed her Captain Grace Flynn, the Crimson Scarver.

Grace had been feared on both land and sea. Then after defeating an evil most foul, she was betrayed by her own allies and brought to this very prison to be hung by her enemies. Perhaps a fitting reward for a woman whom had killed so many without remorse and sometimes reason.

Her mind began to flash the faces of those who had brought her down. She smiled with madness.

"I killed Death and now he comes for me." To any eavesdropper, the statement would have been the raving of a madwoman. Perhaps it was just that, Grace reasoned, and she let the past fade from her mind and shivered slightly as the chill in the air returned. Tears had long left her body and she could not bring forth anymore. Grace's life had been built upon violence and being a slave to a singular thought...vengeance. The dark creature that had taken all from her at such a young age had eluded her and now the sands of her life were running out, never to stand as a monument to her endless rage. She would never kill the beast that slew her family. She would however die upon the hangman's noose. It was only a matter of time.

CHAPTER 1 - THE QUEEN'S REQUEST

BUCKINGHAM PALACE, WESTMINSTER

"Her majesty awaits you in the Yellow Drawing Room." The Queen's guardsman held the palace door open for the stranger dressed in a long brown frock coat. The man eyed the guardsman from underneath his bowler hat and nodded in return. He entered the open door with an elegant stride and heard the door close behind him.

Once inside the man removed his bowler hat and straightened his brown hair by running his hand through it. A footman stood patiently before him as the guest continued to prepare for meeting the Queen. He removed his frock coat and handed it to the footman, along with his hat, the Queen's servant took them both without any word.

"Has the Queen been waiting long?" The guest asked absently.

"I am sure the definition of a long wait would be different for Her Majesty; just know you did take some time to appear in response to her summons. She asked that I bring you to her the moment you arrived." The footman said blankly.

"Well Paris is not exactly a hop, skip and jump, away is it? Well lead on then, I should not keep her majesty waiting any longer." The guest commented.

The pair moved through the low-lit palace and its staff did not even stop their late-night duties to acknowledge the figures as they moved to their destination.

The footman moved at a brisk pace and the Queen's guest had to keep his stride quick to keep up. The pair soon arrived at their endpoint and the footman turned to the man behind him. "I will announce you to Her Majesty please wait here."

The man nodded in return and nonchalantly leaned against the wall in the hallway. He seemed not concerned that he was reclining in the opulent bowels of Buckingham palace. A passing maid snorted and shot her nose up in disdain at his apparent lack of respect. The man raised his eyebrows in mirth and heard the door to the room creak open. The footman stepped out into the hallway and gazed solemnly at the Queen's guest.

"Her Majesty will see you now." The footman eyed the Queen's guest with a haughty glance.

"I am sure she will since I will be standing before her, unless her eyesight has degraded since our last encounter." The man could not resist the quip since he found these royal mannerisms rather boring.

The footman's only response was a wave of his hand indicating that the man should enter. The lavish yellow themed room spread before the man's eyes. Only two figures were in the candle lit room. One was a nervous young chambermaid and the other Queen Victoria herself. Her Majesty was dressed in a rather plain dress considering her status and she paced in front of the low burning fireplace seemingly lost in her own thoughts.

The chamber maid purposely cleared her throat to alert the distracted Queen that her guest had entered.

"Are you sick child?" The Queen said suddenly.

"No, Your Majesty," the maid said with a bow.

"Then don't clear your throat like that on my behalf, I can see he has arrived. Now leave us."

The chambermaid bowed once more and left eyeballing the man suspiciously.

"It would seem your staff is not pleased to see me your majesty," Baron Daedalus informed his host.

"Spare me your observations of my staff Baron Daedalus; you know full well they are not pleased with you over that poltergeist incident."

"I assure you, that monk needed to be dealt with and I am sure your staff did a fine job repairing that room after my encounter with him."

"Yes, they did, and I cannot thank you enough for deposing of that horrid spirit. But I have not called you here to chat about past dealings."

"I assumed that much."

The Queen indicated a nearby sofa and proceeded to sit upon it at one end. Baron Daedalus bowed and sat on the opposite side. The pair sat in silence for a moment, Baron Daedalus could tell the Queen was gathering her thoughts as they passed in twitches of worry across her face.

"What troubles Her Majesty this night?"

"Have you heard of the Ripper?"

"Who in London has not, it has even hit the tongues in Paris as well."

"Then perhaps you have also heard of theorized suspects?"

"If the list is limited to that mentioned in the daily times then I have."

"It is not." The Queen stated in a short tone.

"Then Your Majesty has information that I am not privy to, knowledge I am most likely about to acquire."

Moments of silence once more passed between the pair and Baron Daedalus kindly allowed his host to impart her knowledge in a time and manner as she saw fit.

The Queen's face edged with sorrow and Baron Daedalus saw her stern countenance quiver with inner thoughts. "My own grandson has been placed under scrutiny."

"Prince Albert is an interesting fellow but no murderer." Baron Daedalus pointed out.

"You do not know the depravity my grandson is capable of, and how much of the royal coffers have emptied to keep his indiscreet behavior from the public eye. Baron Daedalus, I know he is somehow connected to this appalling tragedy and I do not need public exposure of his involvement no matter how small it may be."

"I understand your majesty."

"Have you heard of a man named Montague Druitt?"

"Are you implying the Prince is slumming with a supernatural?"

"Then you know of this foul creature and yes the Prince has been spotted entertaining this man at places some men frequent who hold most unnatural desires."

"The Prince's odd sexual frolics even with a Veiler do not put him as suspect for the murder of prostitutes."

"At first glance, you are correct. Yet I personally have had to deal with several extortion attempts by ladies of the night, claiming their bastards were the result of union with my grandson. I dread the thought that these young women of late have died in a most horrific manner to cover the sexual abuses of my grandson in anyway."

Baron Daedalus gazed at a nearby painting of the Queen's family painted many years before and stopped his eyes to rest upon the face of a young boy. The very boy whom they discussed in low voices, now grown into a man and gallivanting about London with a supernatural beast in some kind of hedonistic spree. "I now see your concern. This Druitt fellow does require further examination and I would also assume you want me to clear your grandson of these matters as well."

"You have assumed correct. I called you because you are the only man, I know who can deal with these Veilers or creatures of nightmare."

"Nightmares some may be but most live a life of simple existence."

"Baron Daedalus, I appreciate your observation, but you would not be in such high demand if myth were not real." The Queen said with a slight smirk.

"I too could be also classified as myth and I am quite real and always have been." Baron Daedalus absently noted.

The Queen gazed upon her guest; a stern demeanor once more chiseled upon her face.

"Please do not dander about Baron Daedalus and help the Throne put this delicate matter to rest. You shall find all the appropriate staff at the Yard will not hinder you during this investigation. Also, my personal staff and transports are available for your use, during your investigation. If nothing else at least they might help you be on time in the future."

Baron Daedalus stood and with a bow took his exit from the Queen's counsel. "Good day, Your Majesty."

Baron Daedalus walked over to the door opened it and then slightly turned back to his host. "Once I knew a young Princess who believed in magic and happy endings."

"Happiness seems to be child's play which has come to an end, now that I know how dangerous magic really can be." The Queen said sadly.

"I will find out the truth, Victoria. If there is one thing your old professor knows how to seek, it is the truth."

CHAPTER 2 - THE GOLD
MONT ORGUEIL - ISLE OF JERSEY

Grace Flynn sat with her back against the cold stone walls, her mind drifting into a slight daydream. She could almost hear the waves of the ocean roar and smell the salty air. She would have remained in this blissful moment if not for the clang of iron keys being used to unlock her cell door.

Grace sighed and raised her head to see the door swing open. A pair of French guards entered the room. These particular men carried guns, something out of the ordinary, for all other guards carried only wooden staffs as to not give the prisoners access to guns. The pirate did not stand, she just gazed at the guards with an uninterested look.

Another man entered the small cell, which caused the guards to stand straighter out of respect or maybe fear. Grace knew this man to be Admiral Prideaux, the man who rand a prisoner for one prisoner. Grace could not help but leer slightly at this thought.

"I have come to see if starvation and isolation have finally loosened your tongue, freebooter." Admiral Prideaux informed and continued. "My government is very interested in knowing the location of the wealth you have acquired from us."

"You mean the ill-gotten gold." Grace corrected.

"Regardless of its origin, you Flynn, have stolen something that does not belong you. We simply wish its return, something that may stay your execution."

"You're magnificently dumb, to think I would return your blood money. I killed your navy for it fair and square." Grace spat.

Admiral Prideaux removed his bicorne hat and stroked his dark hair. "This matter will come to resolution before I see your head separated from your shoulders, I assure you."

"So be it." Grace shrugged.

CHAPTER 3 - THE HUNTED

LOZÈRE, FRANCE

Baron Daedalus gazed out the window of his cabin aboard the great airship, Pendragon, he could hear the massive steam powered engines of dirigible hum rhythmically. While down below the French countryside rolled gently about between wisps of gray fog and rain filled clouds.

The vessel was the pride of the English Crown, it was considered to be the finest machine, built and designed by the Tesla & Low engineering firm.

Upon his earlier boarding, Baron Daedalus had mused at the opulence that had been put in for the Queen's benefit and the flaws he saw in the ship's overall design. He quipped with the ship's porter by telling him how he respected his bravery for riding in a vessel that could literally burst into flames under the right conditions. The recipient of his remark snorted in disdain and asked if his passenger would be having any refreshments during the flight. Baron Daedalus had asked for a glass of wine, which he still cradled only half consumed in his right hand.

There was a buzz on the intercom above his head and a voice crackled from it.

"Baron Daedalus, this is Admiral Mark Seagers, Commander of the Pendragon, my apologies for the intrusion, are you there?"

Baron Daedalus grabbed a nearby radio-link device; he turned it on and spoke. "Good Morning, Admiral, I think we can dispense with formalities, while understanding this being the Queen's vessel and I, its only passenger at the moment."

"Fair enough, our arrival time at the Lozere Airport is in about twenty minutes, do you have any requirements other than the vehicle we have radioed for, in preparation for your arrival?"

"No Admiral and thank you for a pleasant flight."

"Glad to be of service, Admiral Seagers...out" The intercom buzzed once more before it closed its connection to the ship's bridge and Baron Daedalus was returned once more to his own thoughts.

The impromptu meeting that was about to take place in a few hours was not something Baron Daedalus was looking forward to. He hated politics and none were more cumbersome than those of the supernatural world.

Montague Druitt was a supernatural and before Baron Daedalus could began a full-blown investigation or sentencing, he would need the approval of the nearest high-ranking Supernatural Council Member, in the vicinity of the illegally alleged activity. Baron Daedalus had tried to reach the local council member, Lord Christopher Vinter at his parliamentary offices, but he was said to be away in France on a recreational hunting trip. Baron Daedalus was well aware of Lord Vinter's supernatural status and also knew that there was much more to his hunting trip than hounds and scarlet coats.

After a rather bumpy landing and a quick chat with Admiral Seagers about his itinerary, Baron Daedalus walked quickly across the airstrip to a group of mechanics and ground crew, who had gathered around a strange looking vehicle in loud conversation.

"Gentlemen, while I would love to answer questions about the design and of my automobile, a pressing matter overrides such frivolity." Baron Daedalus shouted as he brushed through the throng and entered his vehicle. A nearby mechanic gestured to say something, and Baron Daedalus answered him. "Yes, it's a modified Serpolett, I found his original engine to unstable and rather underpowered." Baron Daedalus began the process of starting vehicle up, the machine hissed and sputtered in response. The gathering of observers moved back to give the automobile room to depart and Baron Daedalus shot off when he released the break.

It was not uncommon to be an object of wonderment when driving a steam powered vehicle in the countryside or scaring various animals along the way that crossed in its path.

Inventing such a vehicle had crossed Baron Daedalus' mind many times, however it was far easier to improve on another's work, saving him both time and money lost quite often to prototypes.

The journey to Lord Vinter's estate was uneventful and gave Baron Daedalus time to consider all he learned thus far. He knew that if Druitt was a feral creature, he would hold no life scared and would kill hundreds for pleasure alone, without even a second thought. Baron Daedalus detested the savagery of some Veilers; it was often the cause of many a catastrophe.

Baron Daedalus steered his car to a halt outside the opulent manor. He noticed two other steam cars parked outside, and raised an eye brow observation. Despite their old ways, some Veilers did not shy from innovation.

Perhaps it was their ancient bravado that made them unafraid of change. Baron Daedalus was met by a butler at the manor's entrance who took his coat and hat. He was told that Lord Vinter had received his note and waited for him at the edge of the forest, which extended from the back of the estate. Baron Daedalus was instructed to seek out the stable master for a horse and to ride directly to meet Lord Vinter and his hunting party.

It did not take Baron Daedalus long to do as instructed and within no time he found himself galloping on the back of a fine mare to his host. When he arrived at the hunting party, what greeted him would not have raised any suspicions to an untrained eye. Baron Daedalus knew that the men clad in scarlet coats upon horseback were not the actual hunters. The real hunters were three men garbed in fine dressing robes, and top hats. One of which beckoned heartily to Baron Daedalus. The man was of average height and his face was refined by a well-groomed black goatee, speckled with gray. His eyes were dark and held wildness within them. He was accompanied by two other men with similar facial grooming. Both men appeared to be of English descent.

“Baron Daedalus, your request was urgent, to what do I owe this honor. I assure you neither my guests nor I have broken any Veiled laws.” Lord Vinter flashed a fanged smile and extended a hand to his guest.

“I am aware of this, and may I enquire as to the names of your pack mates?” Baron Daedalus said firmly shaking Vinter’s hand.

“I present Lord Rafe Bentley and Lord Wallace Scott.” Vinter replied, politely waving at each of his guests.

"May I assume that we may discuss Veiled matters in their presence?" Baron Daedalus inquired.

"Lords, Bentley and Scott are my most trusted Pack-Masters, you may speak freely."

Baron Daedalus nodded and explained to the Lords the reason for his visit. The men listened intently and did not interrupt his story.

"Foul business for sure, Baron Daedalus, this Montague fellow sounds uncouth, but claiming him to be Jack the Ripper. That is stretch; no smart Veiler would dare kill so openly." Lord Scott surmised.

"I agree, even though I have seen localized members of my own pack kill without remorse, granted they have been deranged from the start and should have been culled at birth." Lord Bentley added.

A silence hung in the air and then Lord Vinter responded. "Baron Daedalus, long have you upheld the laws of the Veiled people. I know you would not be here unless you had good reason. This stray dog you hunt is not of my pack and pays me no tribute. I have also heard his name whispered in Scotland Yard." Lord Vinter's tone became suddenly cold. "It is best for everyone, if you clear him or kill him before the men of the Yard find out his nature. I need not remind you of the Veiled Laws concerning trial and execution."

"You need not." Baron Daedalus replied.

"Well then hunt away!" Lord Vinter growled.

"It would appear ours is about to begin, Vinter." Lord Scott motioned to a haggard looking man being dragged by a noose about his neck.

"Baron Daedalus, this man was caught killing one of our young. Now he will be executed in our way. This case was already juried by one of your order. You are welcome to ride along for the kill." Lord Vinter said while disrobing and stretching his now nude from.

The other lords followed suit and the prisoner suddenly pleaded to the men for mercy.

"May I enquire as to whom passed verdict?" Baron Daedalus inquired.

"Her name was Baroness Tyri Astrom, I believe. Do you know of her?" Vinter asked.

"Baroness Tyri, is a most honorable Judge and a woman of significant power."

"Will you join us, as we pass sentence?" Lord Vinter said as his body began to spasm. Baron Daedalus watched as the three Lords morphed into huge wolves.

"I shall pass, pressing are my matters at hand." Baron Daedalus stated flatly.

The great wolf who had taken Lord Vinter's place nodded in acknowledgment. It then howled with delight and his packmates joined in.

The prisoner was released and with one last desperate look at Baron Daedalus, who made no move assist him. The man realized his fate was sealed and ran for the nearby woods in escape.

The wolves waited for their prey to get some distance and then yowled as they broke into frenzied pursuit. Tonight, they would feast.

The Veiled laws are clear. If a human kills a Veiler then they shall be killed by one. If a Veiler kills a human, men like Baron Daedalus killed them. Yet as Baron Daedalus watched the wolves enter the forest after the man, he could not help but feel pity, for the man's death would be slow and painful.

Baron Daedalus rode back to Vinter's manor and told the butler he would send word of his findings to Lord Vinter. He then got into his vehicle and began his drive back to the Lozere Airport. The Pendragon would be awaiting him, and he did not want to detain the Queen's vessel any longer than necessary. Besides he needed to find Prince Albert and his companion, tonight.

CHAPTER 4 - DEATH IN THE DARK

MONT ORGUEIL - ISLE OF JERSEY

Grace stumbled backward, her breath was short and rapid as her chest heaved in desperation to take in much needed oxygen. Her hands shook with adrenaline and were covered in fresh blood. All about her cell broken bodies lay motionless cast about like large bloodied dolls. Grace looked at a dead man near her, his head was twisted in an awkward angle and he gazed at up her silently with his lifeless eyes. The other two guards lay in front of her within growing pools of their own blood.

These unlucky guards had come with intentions to rape her, she had defended herself nothing more. The Admiral would not see it that way, he may have even ordered these men to do so, with the hope that she would reveal the location of the gold she had stolen.

Grace laughed and slid down the nearby wall to the floor. She then crawled to the spot where she hid the fragment of her Bloodsilk. Lifting the stone in the floor she pulled it from its hiding place. It suddenly squirmed in her hand as if alive...it was hungry. Death hung in the air, fresh blood was everywhere. Grace could feel the cloth feeding and passing its boon to her. She began to feel clam and refreshed. She could feel her wounds closing and healing. Tonight, Grace would sleep for tomorrow the Admiral would have his revenge for the killing of his guards. But none would attempt to defile her the way these men had failed to do. Fear has a way of making others think before acting. It does not however stop a whip from seeking flesh. The Admiral loved his cat 'o nine tails and Grace knew its sting all too well. Being a prisoner of two nations had its benefits and death by the Admiral's hands without approval was one of them. Grace put her Bloodsilk shard away. Then laid back, closed her eyes and dreamed of her ship...The Lokothea, she could almost smell the sea.

CHAPTER 5 - THE RIPPER
WHITECHAPEL, LONDON

Baron Daedalus had no problem locating the Prince and his associate, despite attempts to conceal their movements. The Prince was quite used to traveling in style, so while he did not use a Palace coach to move about the city, the lavish one he had apparently rented for the night was still out of place within the slums of London.

The pair had spent the beginning of the night crawling through seedy taverns and drinking freely complements of the Palace's coffers. Baron Daedalus was careful to keep his distance and observe his quarry. It was apparent that Montague, was in charge of the duo and the Prince was often compliant to his companion's wishes. Baron Daedalus hoped that tonight's events would involve more than just the consumption of alcohol. If one of these men was indeed Jack the Ripper, he would need them to act upon their twisted desires, if he was to bring an end to the whole sadistic affair.

Upon the strike of the midnight hour, the pair finally made their move and focused their attentions upon a young prostitute named Mary Jane Kelly.

Baron Daedalus had come to know her name and various aliases through conversation with many patrons, and despite her chosen profession, he could understand why some found her attractive. The pale beautiful woman was wholly unaware that her new clients may in fact kill her tonight as she playfully charmed them. If darker events were about to unfold for Mary Jane, Baron Daedalus was powerless to stop them.

The Veiled laws required that a crime must be witnessed for him to exact justice. This was mandated by the High Veiled Council, since many supernatural beings had lost their lives to hearsay or simple, human misunderstanding. As the group left the tavern, Baron Daedalus was careful to keep distance. He followed the trio as they navigated the nearby slums to reach Mary's flat. As they entered her simple dwelling, Baron Daedalus looked for a vantage point to wait out the men as they sought to fulfill their lusts.

The soft glow of candle light appeared dimly warm against the grimy windows of Mary's room. All that Baron Daedalus could see was shadows moving about the inside of the apartment. Hours passed and no screams erupted from within Mary's flat. All seemed quiet and this made Baron Daedalus anxious. Just when he considered moving closer for a better look at the mysterious affair, the door burst open and Prince Albert lumbered out. The man looked ghastly pale and without warning began to retch repeatedly. After he was able to control his stomach once again, Prince Albert frantically gazed about and then darted away from the area, leaving his companion apparently by himself, with their victim. Based upon the Prince's departure, Baron Daedalus was quite sure he would find all the evidence he needed to close the Ripper case firmly.

The scene that opened as Baron Daedalus entered Mary's flat was gruesome to behold. He found Druitt in mid-transformation as he returned to a more human form. The supernatural man made no move to flee. He seemed quite satisfied with himself and his most recent murder as he gazed with content at his unexpected guest.

"I would recommend surrender." Baron Daedalus stated through the handkerchief held over his mouth and nose. The smell of death hung heavily in the air. "This poor girl need not have died for your obsessions, Montague." Baron Daedalus made a mental note to burn his clothing adorned for this evening's romp. The stench of rapidly decaying flesh and blood was hard to mask even with the finest of perfumes. He would never understand these particular creatures and their need to act upon the most carnal of wants. The devouring of a victim's organs to sustain youth while affective for these creatures it did little for intellectual augmentation. One could not simply eat to gain knowledge.

The man named Montague John Druitt, but known to world as Jack the Ripper laughed as he sat nude in a pool of his victim's blood.

"Obsessions, if anyone knows of the power of the great intellectual muse it should be you dear, Baron Daedalus." Druitt's dark eyes burned with madness in the low candle light.

"There is no intellect in murder most foul; of this I can assure you. You have done well in covering your tracks to a point Montague, but you are but a novice in a very old game of hide and seek." Baron Daedalus knew his time for interrogation was running out, it would be only a matter of time before Inspector Abberline and his men, would get word of the murder and move in. “Five women quite a show you have put on for the city, one most will not soon forget and yet your hunger I would assume is far from sated.”

“Are you calling me a glutton?” Montague growled.

“Well if the adjective is correct.” Baron Daedalus did not have time for this feral beast’s tournament of dominance. “Tell me who holds your leash and I can see that you are not put down, like a rabid animal. Her Majesty’s police are not known for kindness in regard to a murderer’s treatment. There is no need for you to die foolishly. “

Montague laughed his face caked with dry blood and bits of flesh. “Did you think I would give up my master’s name so easily?” Another laugh boomed. “Now who is the fool?”

“You still are. Do you not find it disappointing that your master is not here to protect a most loyal servant? Your secrecy only ensures that a life is saved but not yours.”

Baron Daedalus lowered his handkerchief and glared at the creature before him.

“What does your master tell you? There is glory in death. Perhaps honor? Well if that were the case, why do they not give up their life as well and prove it for the entire world to see. You see Montague; there is the great lie you have so willingly become a fool of. You suffer and your master is better for it. Tomorrow they could very well retire from subterfuge and you will still be a dead dog.”

Montague stood, a new found rage making his lithe muscles twitch. He growled his face twisted with a snarl. Even in human form he was still dangerous due to his most recent feeding. The lycanthrope was about to attack when he heard a small buzz and whine from an odd-looking hand gun that appeared in Baron Daedalus’ hand. “Silver infused lightning gun that promises to be effective and most painful. I would sit back down if I were you.”

Montague did not like the doctor's mention of silver and lightening in such close proximity to his naked form. He did not need to be a scientist to know that he had lost tactical advantage.

"Varney." The lycanthrope growled.

"So now the servant knows his master's name. So where do I find, Varney, these days?"

"I do not know. I have only seen him once at my initiation to his order. His commands come by pigeon."

"Pigeon, how inventive and most untraceable," Baron Daedalus deduced with wonder in his voice.

The sounds of the Inspector and his men approaching were apparent to both men in the room. Time had run out and soon the room would be crawling with police. "So, you said you could get my life spared." Montague suddenly pleaded.

"I did. Yet now you are not just some marauding Veiler, you are an uncouth servant of a well-known malignant narcissist. Something I cannot let the good inspector know of." Before Montague could react the crackling of silver lightning filled the air around him as the strange gun discharged. Its spidery effervescence ripped through Montague's exposed flesh. The Veiler felt his heart burst inside his chest as death took him, a look of puzzlement frozen on his face forever.

Moments later...the door to the small flat suddenly burst open and several of Scotland Yard's finest armed with revolvers secured the area.

"Well the battalion has arrived at last." Baron Daedalus raised his hands to show that he was at present unarmed. The officers made no move to search him and brandished their guns to make it clear he would not be leaving anytime soon. The small flat was alive with dismay as the men of Scotland Yard took in the ghastly scene with anguished grunts and faces pale.

"Officers I assure you this crime is not of my doing. Hence there is no blood on my hands nor does any of my clothing expect for my shoes, much like yours, victims in passing alone. There is no way that I could have committed such atrocities and be so impeccably clean."

The men ignored Baron Daedalus' remarks and kept their weapons drawn upon him. Then without warning a young officer retched uncontrollably the murder scene, which was apparently too much for his young eyes.

"Come now surely the Yard's finest have seen blood before. Granted there is quite a bit about and thanks to a weak stomach most of if any scientific evidence contained in said blood is now ruined."

"Look who complains about tampering with evidence a man I do not remember inviting to my crime scene." The husky voice belonged to Inspector Abberline who now stood in the doorway since the flat could not accommodate anymore investigating visitors.

“Inspector perhaps you can have your men be a bit friendlier to a scientific practitioner and agent of the Crown. There is more to this crime than meets the trained eye and it involves things to which my services are required. If your men have the proper clearance, I would be happy to discuss the situation with them as well.”

Inspector Abberline frowned at Baron Daedalus but signaled for his men to stand down. “I want everyone to wait outside, except for you, Baron Daedalus. I expect you men to keep the area outside protected and I do not want any writers or cameras from the local rag snooping about.”

The inspector allowed his men to exit the small grisly flat and proceeded to enter himself and closed the door behind him.

“What exactly would require you to be involved with the Ripper case?” Inspector

Abberline asked as he looked about the room his face scrunching with disgust.

"Why the Ripper himself of course, a personal request from the Queen."

"Do I need to waste time in sending one of my men over to Yard command to verify that statement?"

"Hindrance on your part for this matter does not in the slightest infuriate me; it will however bring the Queen displeasure."

Inspector Abberline gazed back to the corpse on the floor. "Well at least that rabid dog has finally been put down. The real question is where his master is?"

"If you are referring to the Prince, he is long gone. Though I am not so sure that dog was his to control." Baron Daedalus stated flatly.

"Another fine mess you have left for the Yard to cleanup." The Inspector spat.

"I am quite sure this will be a most grateful mess to clean up. I believe your Ripper case has come to a gruesome close." Baron Daedalus continued. "It took me one night to find the lycanthrope that has mocked your precious Yard for weeks now. Mind you, this fellow's imperial entanglements would have proven troublesome to say the least."

"One does not simply question a member of the royal family, even if he is known on the streets to trek with such filth." Inspector Abberline grimaced.

"Correct, now if you require nothing further, I must take leave and continue my investigation, and I would differ any further inquiries about my comings and goings to the Throne itself."

"Tell me, do you hunt these monsters because you are one of them, or is it something else?"

"My dear Inspector, there is at least a mystery the whole of the Yard could never unravel." Baron Daedalus said with a tip of his bowler as he left the Yard to clean up the Ripper's remains.

CHAPTER 6 - THE WICKED HAND
MONT ORGUEIL - ISLE OF JERSEY

The Admiral Prideaux dropped his whip and signaled to a guard near him, the guard brought the admiral a flask of water. The Admiral snatched it and drank until he had completely drained the container.

He then wiped his mouth with his arm and spat suddenly. His shirt was covered in blood and soaked with sweat.

He gazed at a figure hanging from iron chains in the cell. She was unconscious and her back was a bloody mess.

"Leave her a bucket of clean water and fresh clothing. She must look presentable should England come calling to check on her. I have a feeling her wounds will heal as they have before." The admiral then put on his jacket. "I have seen many horrors in this world, but Grace Flynn, is a living curse. We can only hope she is killed soon and before she kills us all." Admiral Prideaux then left Grace's cell.

CHAPTER 7 - DEADALUS' REQUEST
WINSOR CASTLE, BERKSHIRE

Baron Daedalus found that the castle's staff and their opinion of him had improved little since his last encounter with them. He found it amusing however that Queen Victoria's staff was a bit more prudish than the Queen herself was rumored to be. His current guide, a footman, could have been the very portrait of what many considered to be drab. He spoke little and did not seem inclined to answer any of Baron Daedalus' casual inquiries.

The footman somberly led Baron Daedalus to a small library where the Queen sat at an ornately carved wooden desk. She was going over a stack of paperwork. She glanced up, removed her glasses, and met Baron Daedalus with a slight smile. Once the footman had left the pair alone, the Queen spoke.

“My informants tell me the vile companion of my grandson is now expired.”

"That would be a fact Your Majesty."

"My grandson has been persuaded to go abroad, until this matter is over and neatly put away in some dusty file cabinet."

"A wise move Your Majesty."

"What else did you discover?"

"That your grandson's companion was more than just a vile nuisance. He has ties to someone you know quite well."

"And who would that be?"

"Lord Varney Bannerworth."

The Queen raised an eyebrow in shock. She was at a loss for words.

"I too, thought he had expired in that incident at Vesuvius, but it appears he is quite undead."

"This is most disturbing news to say the least, Doctor. I cannot simply list the crimes and troubles that creature has caused this Crown for many generations."

"I am quite aware of Varney's indiscretions and delusions of grandeur. I also know that if he has taken pains to put a supernatural in link to the Crown, he has something rather sinister planned. I imagine he will not be operating alone."

"Whatever do you think this fiend could be up too?"

"I know that he has long sought to repay your forbearers for the actions they took against him both when he was alive, and later when he was undead."

"That creature brought about his own fate, and I personally have done nothing to him."

"The burning of his ancestral home might count as an act against him, and you did have a hand in that."

"True, but my intentions were honorable in seeking to remove that wretched monstrosity off the English countryside and bring the Bannerworth family name back some dignity. If it is not there to be gossiped about, the common people soon forget."

"I understand your actions; however, Varney is not one to let matters rest. I need to stop him before he gets any further along in his twisted scheming." Baron Daedalus leaned forward in his chair emphasizing his next remark. "I need not remind you of the Gevaudan incident, in which your own father had to help the French out of that supernatural debacle."

"What do you think he is undertaking?"

"I am not sure, but the use of a lycanthrope in any matter is messy to say the least. It leads to nothing but exposure in the end or an incident hard to cover from the common folk."

"What is that you need from me Baron Daedalus?"

"I need a new partner."

"Partner," the Queen raised a questioning eyebrow.

"Whatever happened to that nice young lady you traveled with previously?"

"You mean Nasrin Kaur," Baron Daedalus paused as if in deep thought. "She met a fate that even I could not have foreseen."

"That sounds like a fate most unpleasant."

"Yes... but back to the matter at hand, I wish to have Grace Flynn put in my employment."

"Grace Flynn, have you lost your mind? That Sea-Witch is being held prisoner by two nations. Even if I were to release her into your custody, how do you propose to keep a murderess like her under control?"

"Grace Flynn is just the woman I need to handle this particular problem. If I am hunting a killer, it is best I have one on my side."

"Well, you will have that no doubt. Grace Flynn has caused great pains to both the English and French authorities. She is scheduled to be hung within the fortnight." The Queen rubbed her temples as if gathering her thoughts within. "However, you have proven your loyalty and worth to the Crown many times. I will grant this request, but I will hold you responsible for any havoc she creates under your care."

Baron Daedalus quickly added, "I will also require that you clear her of all charges should she prove herself worthy of such reward."

"Grace Flynn, being worthy of absolution? Now here is something even out of your reach. But I do enjoy a good gambit, if you can prove through deed that the notorious Grace Flynn can have a change of heart. Perhaps so shall England, on her lengthy list of crimes. I know most of my advisors would frown upon my next remark, but Grace Flynn has a strength and cunning that even I secretly admire."

"I cannot thank you enough Your Majesty, and I hope that I can stop Varney before he shows us his latest designs."

"Agreed, I will have the papers drawn up right away and you may fetch them tomorrow. You do realize that you must also get the

French government to release her as well. Remember, Miss Flynn is a prisoner of two nations Baron Daedalus."

"Yes, and I do know from a reliable source their current leader is an aspiring inventor. So, I will ask it as a favor from one inventor to another."

"You never cease to confound or charm me, dear Baron Daedalus."

He smiled at her wistfully, "You are, and have always been one of my favorite pupils."

"When we met, I was just a child. Now I am a woman in the winter of her life. Yet you look no older than the first time I saw you."

"You know well of my gifts, we discussed it once before. I cannot age."

"I do not envy you, Baron Daedalus, for there is sadness in the corners of your eyes that perpetual youth can never wipe away."

"How wise of a Queen you have become, and that has nothing to do with our lessons together. We all carry things inside, and often they look out from our souls when we least expect."

"What do my eyes portray?"

Baron Daedalus looked at the Queen with a faint smile. "I see Dash smiling back, Your Majesty."

Tears welled in the Queen's eyes, but she wiped them away with a slight brush of her fingers. "Well I think we have shared enough pleasantries today. May I remind you, Baron Daedalus, a good companion is hard to find among both canines and humans. Treat Miss Flynn with the respect I hope she will earn."

"I shall Your Majesty and Dash was a great and loyal canine, the best any young Princess could ask for."

CHAPTER 8 - NEPTUNE'S STORY
MONT ORGUEIL - ISLE OF JERSEY

Grace awoke to the sound of her cell being opened. She looked up from the floor to see a tall familiar man enter.

"What do you want, your treacherous fop?" Grace asked her visitor.

"I come with a message from England." Nereus Neptune replied.

"Now you are a messenger for the Queen, betrayal has its benefits I suppose." Grace shot back.

"Well Luv...prison has certainly soured your mood."

"Get to the point Nereus before I figure how to break these chains then your neck!" Grace growled.

"I had warned you of the dangers that scarf of yours would lead you to. Grace, you are lucky that England and France did not see you murdered on the spot, upon your capture."

"You are lucky these chains are in the way of me killing you for your part in this."

Nereus removed his hat and rubbed his forehead as if gathering his thoughts.

"I did not come here to bicker with an old friend, who despite her new opinion of me, I still care for very much." Nereus paused and heard Grace huff in disbelief. "A man named Baron Daedalus is arriving soon with an offer you should consider. It will be your last chance to see anything other than you the yard where you shall be hanged...soon I suspect."

"Where are the others?" Grace asked.

“Of Brona and Seaton, I do not know their whereabouts other than they have not been captured. Hate me as you will Grace, they had no part in your capture.” Nereus informed.

Grace slowly sat up, her chains jingling, she heard the Guards outside her cell whisper to each other.

“You have scared them all, Luv, the Admiral may beat you, but none of his men will come near you, they think you are the Devil’s Bride.”

The comment made Grace smirk with delight; her face then turned quickly to a scowl.

“Tell this fellow not to bother coming to see me with his offer, I am ready to meet my fate on my own terms.” Grace stated firmly.

"The Crimson Scarver giving up…No, I think you lack only the motivation to continue this life. I believe this particular man can, perhaps forge your steely resolve into a purpose that will change you for the better and maybe more."

Grace sighed and stretched her arms to the length that her bonds would allow.

"I think it's best you leave and tell your masters to hurry up…I am weary." Grace laid back upon the floor closing her eyes. She then heard Nereus walk off and the cell door slam shut.

CHAPTER 9 - THE INVENTORS
EYSEE PALACE - PARIS

President Sadi Carnot welcomed Baron Daedalus upon his arrival at the President's offices and residence. A courier had arrived hours before Baron Daedalus had landed in the Paris airport alerting the President about him and the meeting he required. After a few moments of formal greetings, the pair moved to Carnot's office to chat further about why Baron Daedalus had sought an audience.

"May I offer you some wine?" Carnot asked his guest as he indicated a leather chair for Baron Daedalus to occupy.

"That won't be necessary Monsieur President." Baron Daedalus replied respectfully.

"Please call me Sadi, I happen to be a great admirer of your work and there is no need to be formal." Sadi invited.

“Sadi, I am sure you are aware why I have requested this meeting.” Baron Daedalus began.

“I know you wish to gain my approval for the release of a most dangerous woman, into your custody. Something the Queen of England, herself, has already done for our shared prisoner.” Sadi added, while his brow lifted in question.

“You are quite correct in your assumptions.”

“Yet the Queen’s backing is not enough to gain my vote of confidence upon the matter.” Sadi paused and sat at his desk across from Baron Daedalus. “You are famous for your works of science and engineering. Many in Paris know of you and your associate, Nikolas Flammel. Yet I feel that there is more to your work than scientific study, hence the reason you are in my office now and requesting things of this nation’s own government. So, Baron Daedalus, if you wish to gain access to Grace

Flynn, you must reveal the other side of your tale." Sadi requested as he sat back and gazed with intensity at his guest.

"I see, are you aware of supernatural beings?"

"Who in Paris has not heard the tales of creatures that haunt our very streets? Most would say this is the talk of drunks and fools. I would disagree. While I have not seen their deeds first hand, I know that there is a part of this world that we have managed or been led to believe does not exist." Sadi replied.

"Have you heard of Protagoras?"

"Concerning the gods, I have no means of knowing whether they exist or not or of what sort they may be, because of the obscurity of the subject, and the brevity of human life." Sadi quoted the philosopher in response.

"It still rings true to my ears, just like the day I heard it from him as he blathered that statement while consuming a most foul-smelling wine." Baron Daedalus remarked.

"Are you implying something?" Sadi asked his faced suddenly pale.

"You wish to know the truth of all things; surely a man who has studied the laws of mechanics knows that there is more to see than what the eye can discern."

"That would mean…" Sadi stammered.

"I am well over two thousand years old," Baron Daedalus informed his host and continued. "Sadi, it is my charge to keep the balance between the worlds of man and the supernatural. The being I now seek to eradicate is extremely dangerous and wishes to harm both England and France for crimes against him. Acts that took place long before you had entered the world with your inquisitive mind. I need a killer to catch one, and Miss Flynn is a perfect fit for my mission."

"It all makes sense now; you are truly the father of invention." Sadi came to full realization as to who his guest was.

“Thank you for your compliment, however I need your help with the matter at hand, so I need you to focus.”

“My apologies Baron Daedalus, the magnitude of your reveal is just overwhelming for a man like me. It was the myths about you that made me seek to understand the nature of things.” Sadi stood and straightened his vest.

“I understand, but what of my request.”

“Your need is most unorthodox and if not for the Queen’s own agreement, I would have refused it. Grace Flynn is a ruthless woman, are you sure you can handle such a person?” Sadi asked.

“Again Sadi, the creature I will ask her to hunt is far more deadly. I would think you should fear for Grace and not me.”

“I do not dread for this woman and if I allow her into your company and she meets an end, then the world is a better place for it.” Sadi retorted.

“If she does not meet this end you speak of and our goal is completed, what shall you do with Miss Flynn?” Baron Daedalus inquired.

“If redemption can be found by Grace Flynn, Then I might exonerate her previous misdeeds. If this does occur and she dares strike against the people of this nation, I assure you that my resolve will be to see her hang.”

“You will not regret this decision, there are events that must not unfold, and Grace is the key to that.” Baron Daedalus stated with resolve.

“I will have the necessary papers drawn up for you right away. The real task you have is to convince, Miss Grace Flynn where her duty now lies.” Sadi paused and smiled weakly. “I am pleased to have gained both knowledge and access to your inner circle. However, Baron Daedalus, even a man of your wisdom and resourcefulness will be putting his life in the hands of a madwoman.”

"If I do survive this course that I have set upon, remind me to tell you about Uther Pendragon, now that is madness." Baron Daedalus retorted.

CHAPTER 10 - THE VISITOR
MONT ORGUEIL - ISLE OF JERSEY

Mont Orgueil's walls cast long shadows in the night as torchlight lead the way for the small party of armed guards and a well-dressed gentleman. The prison did not often receive visitors who were not to remain as permanent guests and even more so at such a late hour.

Baron Daedalus' arrival was quite unexpected and normally would have been turned down if not for the decrees he carried. Baron Daedalus knew he was giving the prison's warden a sleepiness night and he reveled in it, having been an island prisoner once long ago. The memory of that imprisonment also brought a deep pang into the heart and with much effort he sought to suppress the memory at once. Upon his arrival at the interior gates he was greeted by more French soldiers, who knew of his arrival and escorted him to a room where he was held until their Captain arrived. While he waited the guards searched him and found nothing of consequence. Thus, he was considered not be a threat to the prison overall. Baron Daedalus listened to the nearby guardsmen mumble in French about missing a card game to watch over him and about a local tavern named, Le Baiser du Dragon, where the ale and women both had a seedy reputation upon the nearby Parisian coast. Ironically that was Baron Daedalus' next stop, but for more pressing matters than debauchery.

"My apologies, good Baron Daedalus, the Admiral Prideaux requires that all visitors be searched. We live in volatile times, as you are well aware. I must inform you, that the Admiral will not be able to attend tonight's assembly due to an Illness and sends his regards." Captain Blanchard stated and handed Baron Daedalus back his satchel. "We had only just received word from President Carnot and his command that all your requests be adhered to. I will take you to the room where you shall meet the prisoner."

CHAPTER 11 - THE MEETING

MONT ORGUEIL - ISLE OF JERSEY

The large room in which Baron Daedalus was to meet the most dangerous woman alive also served as the dining hall for the prison. All the tables had been cleared away save for one placed in its exact center with only two wooden chairs in attendance opposite each other. Such table arrangements were often considered romantic in other settings, when a man and woman were present together. This was no such affair.

Baron Daedalus took his seat as instructed and opened his satchel pulling out a single dossier. He placed it closed upon the table and waited for Miss Flynn's arrival.

He did not have to wait long. Wooden doors at the opposite end of the hall, creaked open as a large guardsman entered pulling behind him a large iron pole. The strange rod connected to a collar about a shambled looking woman's neck. She was followed by another guardsman of equal size as the first; he held the other end of the shaft. The woman was shackled, and her chains jingled as she was guided to the table.

Underneath her mop of unkempt hair, Baron Daedalus could see that her hazel eyes burned with a silent green fire. She was a spirit unbroken even in this terrible place. Baron Daedalus could not help but feel impressed, after previously reading her file; he knew this woman was something rare.

The guards walked Grace Flynn to the other chair and forced her into it. They remained holding the restraint collar safely out of Grace's reach.

"You must be quite feral to get such large men to take precautions against your claws." Baron Daedalus quipped.

Grace Flynn only glared at her guest and said not a word. Baron Daedalus acted unperturbed by this and opened the dossier on the table, his eyes quickly scanned it.

"Flynn, Grace...born in Wales, daughter of Niles Flynn shipwright and mother, Margaret Brooks, chamber maid. Your father killed during a dock heist and mother died of cholera. You were orphaned at fourteen and were forced into prostitution by a local madam. That led to your association with piracy and to a string of murders numbering potentially in the hundreds; hence you were dubbed the "Sea-Witch". You have been accused of larceny, murder, smuggling, treason and buggery." Baron Daedalus glanced at Grace. "Buggery...You hardly look the type. There is always some sexually repressed lawyer or judge with a latent fantasy. Do you know the whole of society can be broken down into the need of two things, those being sustenance and the other copulation? Here I am straying from the point of my visit. Miss Grace Flynn, I am, Baron

Daedalus, your last chance to ever know freedom outside these walls."

"Whatever government sent you here, you can tell them I have nothing to say." Grace Flynn growled.

"Governments, how many of those must I continually endure?" Baron Daedalus ran his slender fingers through his hair in mild exasperation. "I assure you that I am here of my own capacity and have need of your expertise. It would seem that both governments that you are so inclined to vex over, find you just as maddening."

Grace eyed the Baron Daedalus and considered her response. "So, you don't work for the French or the English and you would have me believe they would just release me to you."

"How awe-inspiring that you are keeping up and I thought this was to be a one-sided conversation." Baron Daedalus quipped.

"Who pulls your strings?" Grace growled.

“I guarantee you Miss Flynn that I am the marionette of none.” Baron Daedalus affirmed.

“You know an awful lot about me, but I have never heard of you.”

“Oh, my dear, you have, though the memory escapes you. I am much like the myths I pursue and eradicate, should that be a necessity. My origins are of little consequence to the matter of your release and future employment. Your cooperation is what must be established at present.” Baron Daedalus opened his leather satchel and pulled out a collection of papers. “You will find these to be a standard contractual agreement from employer to employee with a few amendments to meet the requirements of your imprisoning governments and to meet my own requests as well. “

“Contract… Are you bloody serious?” Grace laughed.

“Quite serious, the contract is also for your benefit. It states that by serving as my associate, the governments who hold you prisoner, will lessen your sentence or quite possibly dismiss all of your current charges based on my reports of your actions while under my employment. There is also the matter of reimbursements for any services you provide me, for which I find to be satisfactory."

"I am no whore if that is what you are after!" Grace spat.

"I have read your dossier and know quite well how you deal with interests of unwanted affections. In fact, it's your tenaciousness and sheer defiance in the face of insurmountable odds that I find most delightful. For what I will ask you to face while under my employment would make most women swoon with fear. I am quite sure Miss Grace Flynn that you have looked in the eyes of death and smiled. Just be advised by entering this contract that one day it just might smile back. I would like to point out there is a clause for proper disposal of your body should it be possible considering the circumstances of your demise while in my service. I also provide a letter to any relatives of your choosing letting them know you did not suffer at the end and will opt a more plausible end that a commoner may understand."

"You are absolutely bonkers. Who are you? I do not have time for games even in this place."

"I assure you Grace Flynn this is no game. You can take this offer of employed freedom or rot in a cell in the middle of the ocean as two governments fight over who will carry out your sentence. I offer you a chance to prove that are you are more than a scallywag and that you can make a difference. I also offer you a chance to work with me, an opportunity many in this world would never pass up."

"You seem quite sure of yourself."

"Yes I am."

"There is just one problem with your contracts; I will not sign them willingly."

"Hmm…a most unfortunate problem for you, yet my offer still stands. Work for me and freedom might one day be yours."

"How do you know that if I do sign and leave with you. That I do not run away or simply just kill you?"

"Many have tried, so your attempt would just be old hat. There are things and places in this world you will see in my company that shall amaze and terrify you. Also, once you get to know me better and see my work you will never want to leave contract or not. So, let us dispense with needless banter and let's have your signature on these forms."

"Baron Daedalus, the freedom you offer is worthless. I am weary of this world and will accept my fate." Grace replied calmly.

"There is one other thing I can offer you…revenge."

"Revenge…Against my enemies?" Grace laughed.

"No revenge, for your father, the only man you have ever loved."

"My father died in a shipping accident!" Grace growled, while her guards drew their pistols upon her back.

"You know that is not true. He was, as you have long suspected, the victim of a vampire's wrath" Baron Daedalus responded and waved the guards back.

"Now you prove yourself to be crazy, by blathering about vampires!" Grace spat.

"It is known that vampires often haunt the brothels for virgin blood. If one were to consider your past, one can assume you know quite well that I am not blathering." Baron Daedalus could see emotions stir in Grace's visage. "Did you long for the creature that killed your father to seek your own neck for pleasure, so you could kill him?" He allowed his previous statement to settle in his listener's mind. "Not the thing that most young girls forced into prostitution would hope for, but you, Grace

Flynn, are something more than a forgotten flower."

Grace said nothing in response her eyes however did narrow. Baron Daedalus assumed she was now calculating her next move.

"I understand this is all very hard to take in and I know you are not one who gives trust so easily. I need your help in as much as you need mine. Your life has been adrift Grace Flynn, its time to hunt with purpose and track down this creature you have long sought."

Grace still did not respond.

"Please understand me when I say this, once long ago I was a prisoner too, I felt betrayed and angry while my enemy remained at large." Baron Daedalus paused. "The being you seek is called Varney, and he has killed more young women than any other monster in history. Now he seeks to potentially kill possibly thousands of people in one fell swoop. There is young girl right now in her father's arms that will remain safe, if you go with me now and stop this monster's designs."

"Freedom and revenge," Grace stated flatly. "Well Baron Daedalus if you wish me to sign your little agreement, I will need to be unshackled."

"Gentlemen you may leave the keys to release the prisoner and make a way for her exit."

Baron Daedalus commanded as he stood. He then asked for his coat and bowler to be retrieved.

Baron Daedalus unshackled Grace Flynn and she rubbed her wrists rhythmically. She then reached for the fountain pen. Her hand closed on it like a blade. Slowly her hand rose to a stabbing position. She eyed Baron Daedalus who simply glared back. Higher her hand rose; the guards of the prison watched the scene unfold. Then Grace changed her grip and in one fluid motion signed the contract with a zealous flair.

"Now that you are under my care and employment, we must get you cleaned up right away. Prison has not done you well." Baron Daedalus smiled.

Soon Grace donned Baron Daedalus' bowler and overcoat and the pair were escorted out of the prison. When they arrived at the harbor a dirigible awaited them just off the coast, and for the first time in many months Grace inhaled fresh salty air. Baron Daedalus motioned to a rowboat just off a nearby dock. The pair boarded it and they rowed out to the Pendragon and then climbed up a rope ladder to the passenger cabin area. After they boarded the vessel hummed to life and began its journey to Paris as instructed by Baron Daedalus.

"This vessel is amazing." Grace remarked absently.

"Grace from this point onward you must adhere to my commands both our lives depend on it." Baron Daedalus said firmly.

"You get me to the beast that killed my kin and I will do the rest, problem solved, world saved."

"If it were only that easy," Baron Daedalus replied.

CHAPTER 12 - THE DRAGON'S MIST

LE BAISER DU DRAGON - PARIS

Baron Daedalus and Grace entered the smoke-filled tavern and none of its patrons bothered to look their way. It did not take long for Grace to realize the purpose of the establishment.

"I told you that I am not a whore!" Grace hissed as she gazed threateningly at her new employer.

"Calm yourself, Grace, a reward still exists for your capture in more unscrupulous circles. This establishment is where we shall get clothing for you and I need to speak with its Madame, regarding a most vital situation." Baron Daedalus whispered back.

The barkeep of the establishment was a large African man who motioned for the pair to come closer. "We are not buying any girls tonight." The man informed them.

"I am not here for that Leone. I do however need to see Madame Woo, please tell her Baron Daedalus is here." Baron Daedalus said removing his bowler and moving into the nearest light source.

"My apology, I will summon Madame Woo." The great man lumbered away and left Baron Daedalus and Grace at the bar.

"There is something you must know about our host. She is a Veiler and a creature of immense beauty and death. Outwardly she is just a woman, until she lets her hair down." Baron Daedalus momentarily paused, as he calculated his statement. "She will know who you are so there is no need to use your cover name; we would only insult her by doing so."

Grace nodded in response and pulled the overcoat she wore tighter about her body. "This woman sounds coldblooded."

"Your statement is truer than you know."

It did not take Leone long to return and he motioned for them to follow. He led the pair down a winding hall to a great room at the back of the building. A perfumed smoke swirled in its interior as gaslights flickered along its exterior walls. A great dais was at its back and a woman sat upon a golden throne. She placed the hookah down, that she was smoking and stood.

Even in the low light Grace could tell this woman was beautiful. There was also a feeling of sensuality that hummed in the very air. It grew stronger as she approached them; she sauntered over and instantly embraced Baron Daedalus. Her eyes fell upon a Grace and she swore that the woman licked her lips, or perhaps tongue flickered. Grace noted the woman was of Asian heritage, but her accent was Parisian.

“So, the rumors are true, the great Grace Flynn has left her little cage.” Madam Woo cooed. “What have you gotten yourself into now Baron Daedalus?”

“I am not here to be interrogated. I came by your request and also require your help.”

Baron Daedalus stated and politely escaped the Madame's embrace.

"All business today we are?" Madame Woo toyed.

"What is it you wish to tell me?" Baron Daedalus asked.

"Several days ago, a shipment of commodities came into port and proved to be a bit of an issue for me. Since I do not need the eyes of Veiled Council upon me, I contacted the one human for the job. My entire cargo was destroyed; all I am left with is a problem." Madame Woo confided.

"You need not be so vague Woo; Grace is in my employment and should be granted access to all information." Baron Daedalus informed his host.

"All Information..." Madame Woo hissed then without warning her hair began to writhe. The sounds of scales rubbing together, and the hiss of serpents sang loudly. Grace looked in shock at the woman's mane of living serpents.

“Do I frighten the great Crimson Scarver?” Madame Woo purred sarcastically.

“Serpents are only a problem when close enough to bite.” Grace shot back.

“Woo, I do not have time for your syncopations of control. I need to know what you have uncovered. My hope is that it does not connect to my current errand.”

Madame Woo’s hair settled once more to a more human fashion, and she reached out and rang a nearby gong with her closed fist. It only took a few minutes of awkward silence before Leone appeared and bowed to his Mistress.

“Take these two, to the vermin.” Madame Woo commanded.

Leone bowed once more and motioned for Baron Daedalus and Grace to follow. The trio navigated the establishment until they came to a trapdoor in the kitchen. Leone opened the door and a ladder was beneath. He grabbed a lantern that hung within and lit it. He then descended the steps with Baron Daedalus and

Grace in tow. The stepladder led down to a vast wine cellar and at its rear was an iron gate. Something beyond it moaned in agony.

"What is in there?" Grace questioned.

"Zombie," was Leone's solemn reply.

Baron Daedalus paused knelt suddenly and retrieved a small pistol from a holster strapped to his ankle. "Just precaution I assure you," He said with a weak grin.

"I feel safe now." Grace mocked.

Leone stopped at the door and held up the lantern. Pale sickly hands burst through the iron bars, while a gruesome and hallowed face roared in frustration being denied a chance to greet its guests properly. The creature's dead eyes leered and oozed with decay. Baron Daedalus heard Grace gasp in shock, like most humans did when they saw the undead for the very first time.

"How long has it been here?" Baron Daedalus asked.

"Three days, Woo had it brought here when we found it, aboard the ship along with the others."

"Others...and, where are they?" Baron Daedalus inquired.

"Woo's warehouse on the Paris docks. Fear not we have taken measures to contain them properly until your arrival. The Madame wants you to fix the problem before the Veiled Council finds out." Leone banged the iron door as the creature continued its desperate attempt to grab anything living.

"Who is the Vampire responsible for this?" Baron Daedalus asked knowing that no answer was forthcoming.

"Unknown, the infection was done at sea." Leone answered.

Daedalus nodded. He then motioned for Leone to open the door.

"Have you lost your mind? That thing looks hungry." Grace yelled.

"Well then this should be quick." Baron Daedalus shot back. He waved at Leone again to release the creature. The large man kicked the iron bars and the Zombie backed up in response. He then unlocked the door and stepped aside. The creature within needed no cue as it blasted through the doorway as the gate slammed open. Before it could reach Baron Daedalus, his pistol exploded, the Zombie's head flung backward, and it toppled to the floor motionless.

"Dispose of it as required. I will see myself and Grace back to Woo. I need more answers." Baron Daedalus commanded.

Leon nodded and he then reached for a nearby hatchet and set to work. Grace heard the blade sever flesh and bone. She did not need to look back to know the creature was being dismembered.

"This is madness; perhaps I was safer in prison." Grace laughed.

“Perhaps you were, but now there is turning back.” Baron Daedalus said as he cleared the top of the ladder.

The pair returned to Madame Woo’s chambers. Before Baron Daedalus could speak, two scantily women entered the room behind them.

“Ladies please see that my guest,” Madame Woo paused and gazed at Grace. “Is bathed and dressed properly in dress befitting a lady.” Madame Woo commanded.

The women giggled and walked over to Grace taking her by the hands. Baron Daedalus waved Grace to go with them.

“A Zombie…You know this is a very serious matter, I will however not alert the Veiled Council at this time. I will need to destroy the others immediately.” Baron Daedalus began to pace back and forth in apparent thought.

“I assure you Baron Daedalus I was not the cause of the calamity and loss several young flowers to those creatures. I know you do not approve of my dealings, but this is not of my design."

"I know this was an act of supernatural terrorism. Someone my have begun their machinations against their enemies." Baron Daedalus concluded.

"Who has begun this?"

"That is not for your knowledge, my dear Woo."

"First I lose my valuable cargo and now you keep secrets from me." Madame Woo sulked.

"I think it is for the best. Is my car here?" Baron Daedalus asked.

"Yes, it is behind the building. That friend of yours is a most handsome fellow and much more playful than you." Madame Woo teased and moved closer to her guest.

"Flammel is a man of his own means and I am not his keeper."

“He tastes like you…why is that?” Madame Woo inquired.

“So, you have fed on him too? That is something of another matter, one that I cannot discuss.” Baron Daedalus answered.

“So many secrets for the man, who has lived so many lives,” Madame Woo smiled knowingly.

Grace returned with her escorts and was dressed in a dress befitting any young woman who graced the Parisian streets on holiday.

“What?” Grace growled; she did not appear to enjoy the gawking she was receiving.

“Who could have guessed this particular woman could be so intoxicating. You could steal the very Devil’s heart, now I see why you were so successful at your vocation.” Madame Woo remarked.

“Yes, Miss Virginia O’Connor is quite fetching. Thank you very much ladies.” The escorts left the trio alone.

“Now tell me where to find your warehouse.” Baron Daedalus demanded.

Madame Woo did as she was asked and minutes later Baron Daedalus and Grace were racing through the streets of Paris in his steam car. Grace seemed to enjoy the ride and commented that Baron Daedalus must teach her to drive, in case he was incapacitated and unable to operate the vehicle. Baron Daedalus only glowered in response.

CHAPTER 13 - TO EARN ONE'S KEEP
LE HAVRE PORT - PARIS

Baron Daedalus and Grace had no problem in locating the warehouse to which they were sent. The building was old but did show recent repairs to both its roof and the large entryway with its double doors, which were sealed with a heavy iron chain.

"Normally a lock of this sort would protect something very valuable from the unscrupulous dock workers; in this case they are being protected from what's inside." Baron Daedalus Observed.

Grace looked about while the afternoon sun was beginning to wane and anxiously fidgeted with the fine dress she wore, in obvious discomfort. "Are we going find another one of those Zombies in here?" She asked with a hopeful tone.

"Are you that excited about the prospect of killing?" Baron Daedalus quipped.

"I am eager to be done with this whole weird affair and kill my father's murderer, if you must know." Grace shot back.

Baron Daedalus knelt and began looking within the bag he had brought with him from the steam car. He pulled out a pair of pepper-boxes and motioned to Grace with one, to come over. Grace complied and took the guns from him, along with the reserve rounds and examined them.

"These are modified from the ones you are used to wielding. Each will fire six shots before you have to reload, and I suggest you use them with accuracy." Baron Daedalus stated as he held similar weapons. "Madame Woo indicated there are at least a dozen Zombies within this facility. Under no circumstances must any escape, they are going to be quite hungry and we need not worry about finding them."

"Sounds like fun." Grace mocked.

"You must aim for the head to incapacitate the creatures. Once we have taken them all down. We will decapitate them all and burn the bodies."

"How gruesomely efficient you are. Is there anything else I need to know about these monsters?"

Baron Daedalus pulled the chains securing the doors off. "Aim for the head and don't miss!" Without another word Baron Daedalus swung open one of the great doors. A foul smell overtook the pair as Baron Daedalus used a nearby lever to ignite the gaslights in the warehouse. The illumination above hummed and hissed to life. As the shadows melted away, a ragged group of horrific beings lumbered toward the entrance of the warehouse.

Baron Daedalus nodded and rushed forward. Grace followed suit and began to fire upon a pair of Zombies that took interest in her. Her skill with the pistol was uncanny as her first two shots dropped two Zombies to the floor. She did a quick glance about and counted about ten more of the creatures which did not include the trio, which Baron Daedalus had just expended.

Pistols blazed as Zombies fell like broken rag dolls. Soon all the lumbering creatures were scattered about the warehouse floor.

“That was not so bad.” Grace laughed.

“Something is not right.” Baron Daedalus stated somberly.

“I don’t follow, we came to kill them and now we are done.”

“You don’t understand, they should have set upon us likes rabid wolves. Something is feeding on them.” Baron Daedalus said in realization.

Before Baron Daedalus could explain a great scuttling, sound rose as a giant arachnid appeared before them.

“Don’t move a muscle, it is attracted by movement, the Cave-Leech Spider is blind. They were used by some Vampires to keep predatory animals away from their natural crypts." Baron Daedalus stood perfectly still, and Grace quickly followed suit.

"Woo, forgot to mention her little pet!" Grace hissed.

"We will be forced to kill the creature, there is no alternative. I will fire upon it, when I do so, aim for its underbelly and blast away."

Grace needed no further instruction.

Baron Daedalus fired off a few rounds and the great arachnid shot toward him and raised its front legs, while its fangs clicked angrily at him. Grace saw her opportunity and fired her remaining rounds in a great volley. The creature shrieked and backed away, it turned to weakly run but soon slumped to the floor its wounds oozing.

"This was a trap; Woo did not neglect telling us about this creature." Grace remarked.

"I would have to agree with you. It would appear Madame Woo was looking to collect upon your bounty with those who operate outside the law. This little problem has cost her much and gold does strange things to anyone." Baron Daedalus knelt to examine a nearby Zombie. "These sailors and not of Parisian origin." He pulled a bloody rosary from the corpse. "I would say somewhere in Italy is their home port. Italian sailors often carry rosaries blessed by the Pope for long journeys at sea."

"How did they get like this?" Grace asked.

"That is a question I cannot answer just yet. I will need a sample of blood. Please help me drag the bodies into a pile of sorts outside. I will do the bloody work while you look for something to ignite them with."

It was after nightfall when Daedalus had completed his work and set the corpses to flame. He then gathered his belongings and headed for the steam car.

"Are we just going to leave this blaze?"

"There is no time and no imminent danger of it spreading beyond the bodies. The local authorizes will consider it some sick gang warfare, case closed." Baron Daedalus replied chillingly.

Grace did not push the matter and ran after her employer as fast as her current garb would allow. They got into the car and drove away.

"We are off to my associate; he knows your identity. You will also see things most unordinary please refrain from questioning him. I need him to sample this blood I have collected."

"I understand…unordinary you say, I know nothing about that after today's events so far." Grace retorted.

CHAPTER 14 - NIKOLAS FLAMMEL
LE MARIAS, PARIS

Nikolas Flammel was a dashing man, well-groomed and much warmer than Baron Daedalus in his mannerisms. Grace felt a sudden comfort with the man who welcomed them both heartily.

"Miss Flynn, your deeds are most fascinating, and your scarf is something of a wonder." Flammel stated as he guided her to his laboratory underneath his posh townhome.

"What do you know of my scarf?" Grace snatched her arm from his and glared. Daedalus shook his head disapprovingly at Flammel.

"I have been examining a small piece if it for many months. Its properties are almost life like in nature." Flammel added.

"The scarf has been locked away in a very safe place and will not be returned to you, Grace. It is an entity of evil and there will be no more discussion about it." Baron Daedalus revealed and motioned for the pair to follow.

"That is my property and I want it back!" Grace demanded.

"It is my job to ensure that entities of the Veiled are not harming humanity. That item was harming you and it will no longer." Baron Daedalus turned. "You are remembering only the power it gave for the lives that you took without remorse.

This is why I chose you Grace; your murderous spree was not of truly of your own design. In much the same way, an opium addict can't control their own urges once the dragon has them."

Grace considered what her employer stated and grunted with dissatisfaction. She stormed to Baron Daedalus and her fists clenched.

"Don't let your latent addiction ruin this opportunity you have Grace. Take breath and know I have your best interest at heart." Baron

Daedalus walked away into the Flammel's laboratory. The room was huge considering that it was underground. Instruments and machines buzzed and hummed all about as a great water wheel spun rhythmically powering the entire facility. In its exact center a large glass tank was filled with pale blue water and something floated within it. As Grace got closer, she saw what it was. A pale and nude woman floated, gently asleep in the tank, her mouth connected to a tube that rose to the water's surface. Bubbles escaped with each breath she took. Grace was both amazed and shocked.

"Her name is Esmeralda, and she is my wife." Flammel said with sadness. "She is a Dhampir, child of a Vampire and a human. She asked to be put into this stasis until I was able to find a cure for her Vampirism. One does things sometimes that don't make sense to those outside the grip of love."

"I will not pry into this anymore, Flammel your affairs are yours." Grace said respectfully.

Baron Daedalus explained the reason for his visit to his associate who listened keenly and did not interrupt. Once the tale was told, Flammel took a moment to consider all he heard.

"Let me examine the blood against the samples I have." Flammel took the sample from Baron Daedalus and began working on it.

Baron Daedalus saw Grace once again gazing at Esmeralda. "She is a wonderful woman, and once was my greatest companion. Much like you she was possessed of a fire that could not be quenched, unless revenge was dealt for the atrocities put upon her." Baron Daedalus disclosed to his new companion.

"Will I seek solace in a jar too when you have finished with me?" Grace said.

"I think not Grace, you are human, something, Esmeralda would envy you for." Baron Daedalus remarked.

Flammel returned from his work and handed Baron Daedalus a chart. "This venom belongs to a priest?" Baron Daedalus looked puzzled.

Flammel was about to respond when a buzzer rang out. He walked over to a console and flipped a lever. "May I ask who is calling?"

There was a static growl and then a voice sounded. "My Name is Father Jacob Knoxx, I am from the Holy See and need to speak with Baron Daedalus, and my representatives tell me he is here."

Flammel shrugged at Baron Daedalus.

"Let us not keep the Pope's man waiting." Daedalus answered.

CHAPTER 15 - POPE'S REQUEST

LE MARIAS, PARIS

Baron Daedalus and his companions received their guest in Flammel's library. The man's accent was flat, and Grace could not point out his heritage. After a few minutes of formal introductions, he stated the reason for his visit.

"The Holy Father has sent me on a most grave mission. It has come to light that priests of smaller parishes in Rome have gone missing. These particular men of the cloth are Veiled citizens, they are also extremely loyal to the church." Father Jacob revealed over a freshly poured glass of tea.

"Is the Holy Father also aware that Varney is not eliminated as once believed?" Baron Daedalus questioned his guest.

"I cannot say, but if that is a true statement then these missing priests are in danger." Knoxx's tone was very serious. "There is no time to waste; you must speak to the Holy Father right away. I will leave your company now and make arrangements for the meeting" Knoxx paused and glanced at Grace. "Reports say this woman is dangerous, The Holy See does not approve of your choice in her as a companion. I only hope you know what you are doing." The priest said nothing further and Flammel escorted him out.

"How dare he pass judgment on me," Grace barked.

"He is only stating observations on your well-known crimes." Baron Daedalus replied.

Grace was about to respond when Flammel walked back in. "I shall pack my instruments. Also, Grace you should accompany me. Esmeralda is about your size and I have in storage some of her old clothing and gear, which will suit you better on this journey than that dress."

Grace did not need another invitation and quickly followed Flammel.

An hour has passed since Knoxx's departure and Grace now dressed in clothing suited for an expedition and a pair of tall leather boots, felt more relaxed. Both of her companions complimented her on her choice of apparel.

"I find it interesting that a legendary murderesses' beauty is just incomparable." Baron Daedalus smiled.

"Watch yourself boss." Grace shot back.

"I mean that in the most platonic of ways. I assure you."

"If you two are finished sparring, I do have work to complete outside of this unexpected adventure." Flammel grumbled as he loaded his bags in the steam car's trunk.

"Cheer up Flammel, after all, the Queen herself has provided our means of passage." Daedalus winked as he sat behind the wheel and fired up the engine. Soon enough the steam car was barreling toward the Paris Airport.

CHAPTER 16 - THE HOLY SEE
BASILICA OF SAINT JOHN LATERAN, ROME

Pope Leo XIII awaited Baron Daedalus and his companions surrounded by his closest advisors. The Cardinals each greeted the party respectfully as they entered the Conclave hall. Even Grace was treated with respect despite her scandalous reputation. After the introductions, the group sat at a large wooden circular table that appeared to be ancient, which accommodated exactly thirteen seats comfortably. Each seat was marked with a heraldic symbol, except the Pope's which was marked with a golden crown. Baron Daedalus and his companions were seated between various Cardinals, in extra chairs.

"My advisors tell me that you have news about the missing Vampires and the one called Varney, once believed to have been exterminated by you." Pope Leo began the discussion. He then frowned when he noticed

Grace not paying attention. Baron Daedalus had noticed Grace looking intently at the table at which they were seated.

"Yes, it's the Round Table, of Arthur and the sight of the Last supper as well. Now please pay mind to the conversation and to the Pope when he speaks." Baron Daedalus whispered to her quickly.

"My apologies Your Eminence, my companion was distracted by the beauties of your hall. Let me begin by stating that a ship bound for Paris, had Zombies aboard of Italian heritage. The venom used in their creation was found to be that of a Vampire most likely on the list of your missing priests. Also, it has come to light that Varney may indeed be once again at large. It would seem he has chosen to repay England and France for their quarrels with him." Baron Daedalus summarized.

The Cardinals began to whisper to each other and soon words fell upon the Pope's ears. Pope Leo XIII listened to the Cardinals seated on either side of him and then spoke. "This is news most disturbing. It is also a problem that the Church cannot resolve. You, Baron Daedalus must resolve this matter discreetly and with haste."

"I will your Eminence, but first I need to know which of your Vampires disappeared first." Baron Daedalus inquired.

The Pope and his council of Cardinals gave Baron Daedalus all the information they had in regard to the matter at hand. He listened intently doing his best to be polite where he was required by Church etiquette. Grace however was beginning to get bored and if not for Flammel's company the ex-pirate would have started to consider how she could plunder all the riches within sight. The companions soon left the Pope's council to rest in a local hotel and finalize a course of action.

CHAPTER 17 - FANGED MYSTERY
ROME

"The Catholic Church is quite full of Vampires that is a rather unexpected twist." Flammel stated flatly.

"It would be since it was founded by one." Baron Daedalus added.

"Well that is just blasphemy, Baron Daedalus." Grace laughed.

"No, it is not. The one called Christ was indeed a Vampire, in fact so were his twelve disciples at least after the famous Last Supper and the Vampire blood ritual. I should also note that two of the original Apostles were in attendance at our meeting with the Pope. They were the Cardinals that sat on either side of His Eminence." Baron Daedalus offered.

"The real question here is what Varney is up to. How can he attack two separate countries?" The Alchemist deliberated. "It would take a vast army something he does not have." Flammel reasoned aloud.

"That's it he does not need to build a vast army when he can have it replicate itself." Baron Daedalus realized. "Italian ship was not an attack; it was an experiment."

"Are you saying he plans to release Zombies in both Paris and France?" Flammel asked.

"It's the only way this particular devil could ever create an army. It is also the reason he has kidnapped so many Vampires."

CHAPTER 18 - A MESSAGE
ROME

The companions awoke the very next morning and made their way back to the Roman airport. The Pendragon was still docked there under instruction and the Admiral had used the time to perform maintenance upon his vessel.

Baron Daedalus gave the Admiral a letter to wire to England to update the Queen on his progress. After that he boarded the Pendragon joining Grace and Flammel in the passenger cabin.

Grace looked at Baron Daedalus and then to Flammel, “So what now are we to sit here and wait for post from the Queen?”

Baron Daedalus smiled and then stood. “I think it’s time we took the sights and see what the locals know of our little problem.”

"Never seen Rome...this should be fun." Grace stood and motioned for the Baron to the lead the way.

CHAPTER 19 - VENETIAN VAMPIRES

VENICE, ITALY

Despite the reason for being there, Grace found the city of Venice extremely beautiful. She and Baron Daedalus had spent the first day of their arrival trying to gather any intelligence regarding any strange Veiled activity within the floating city. She encountered various beings; Vampires, Werewolves and even a Selkie. Grace silently had wished the beautiful young woman had turned into a seal, just so she could see the transformation.

It almost appeared as if they had hit a dead end, until one day while enjoying a quite lunch at an outdoor café. The sound of a rifle broke the afternoon air. The glass of wine Baron Daedalus was about to drink exploded in his hand.

Grace Sprung to her feet and pulled out her pepper-boxes. She scanned the area looking for the point of the slug's origin. Baron Daedalus suddenly shoved her out of the way as another shot screamed between them. Baron Daedalus pointed to a nearby rooftop. Grace glanced upward to see a woman garbed in black military dress and a matching top hat reloading her rifle.

"Who the hell is that and why is she trying to kill us?" Grace screamed as the other patrons and café staff rushed for cover.

"Nasrin Kaur, my pervious companion and she is not trying to kill us. She is warning us to stay away. Trust me she does not miss when she wants to claim a target." Baron Daedalus replied through the chaos around them.

"I thought your previous companion was dead." Grace stated standing once more.

"It would seem some people are not inclined to die." Baron Daedalus spat.

The woman called Nasrin Kaur, gave Baron Daedalus a long glance from her position and then leapt out of sight.

"Do we chase?" Grace asked.

"No, she will be long gone, and the next time we meet she will not fire a warning shot."

CHAPTER 20 - CONFESSION

VENICE, ITALY

After several days of continued hunting for answers the companions were rewarded by capturing one of Varney's agents who had been sent to tail them. He was young for a Vampire and a bit overzealous about his assignment.

They learned from the Vampire named Giorgio that Varney was in Venice and was creating Zombies as Baron Daedalus concluded. The prisoner also revealed that Varney was planning to use a dirigible to drop those Zombies throughout England and France in densely populated areas. The vessel was currently in docked in outside San Giorgio Maggiore and fuel was delivered to it by gondola. Once they had extracted all the information they could from the Vampire, Baron Daedalus executed him for crimes against the Veiled.

Grace was shocked to learn the cold demeanor her employer sometimes held. She had no love for Vampires but watching Baron Daedalus execute one did seem a bit odd.

"The Veiled laws are clear; conspirators against humanity must be killed." Baron Daedalus told Grace as he lit the gondola that held the Vampire's corpse. Slowly the vessel slid out to sea.

CHAPTER 21 - FLIGHT
SOMEWHERE OVER ITALY

The next day Baron Daedalus and his companions were taken by boat out to the Pendragon that had arrived over night to assist in the hunt for Varney. When they boarded, Baron Daedalus relayed all he knew about the dirigible to Admiral Seagers.

"I believe that I saw that very blimp leave an hour ago flying west. I assumed it was just a shipping vessel out for delivery. I do believe we can catch it." Admiral Seagers advised. "I will get us underway. Also, the equipment you requested is aboard. I am very interested in seeing those machines in action."

"What machines is he talking about?" Grace asked.

"Icarus Gliders, a set of mechanized wings that will help us get aboard Varney's vessel." Baron Daedalus answered.

“We are going to fly!” Grace squealed quite suddenly.

Baron Daedalus and Flammel looked at each other in confusion in response to Grace’s outburst. Grace rolled her eyes at both of them and began preparing her weapons for the attack.

“Just to be clear...Varney is mine.” Grace said loading her pepper-boxes.

“We will have to get through Nasrin first I believe and that will not be easy.” Baron Daedalus added.

“What part will I play in this endeavor?” Flammel asked. “I am not suited for combat as you well know Baron Daedalus.”

“No one is asking you to commit to such; you will remain on the Pendragon and help the Admiral keep his ship in the air if that is required.” Baron Daedalus stated.

“That I can do,” Flammel saluted.

CHAPTER 22 - ICARUS WINGS
SOMEWHERE OVER ITALY

The Admiral did as he promised and within an hour of their departure, The Pendragon rose up behind Varney's dirigible.

The ship's intercom crackled to life. "We are now upon the vessel. You must depart now before we are discovered." Admiral Seagers informed his passengers.

Baron Daedalus helped Grace put on a leather and metal backpack. It weighed more than it appeared. He donned a similar one and then gave Grace Instructions for the use of the equipment.

"The crank in the center of your chest will release the wings; you must turn it once you have jumped from the ship. You steer but twisting your shoulders left or right and by lifting your shoulders up or down." Baron Daedalus drilled.

Grace nodded that she understood. Without further chatter, Baron Daedalus walked over to a trap door in the passenger cabin. He opened the door and leapt into it. Grace could not help but gasp and she quickly gazed out the cabin's windows to see Baron Daedalus soar by the windows and to Grace and Flammel, he resembled a giant bird. Grace could not contain her excitement and jumped into the open trap door, like a pirate boarding another vessel. Flammel soon saw her swoop by the windows as well. For a moment he felt a pang of jealously, but then he remembered how much he liked his feet on the ground.

CHAPTER 23 - STRANGE BIRDS
SOMEWHERE OVER ITALY

The strange birds that were indeed Grace and Baron Daedalus encountered no trouble as they reached the dirigible and quickly boarded it from the back using an unprotected cargo door. They quickly learned why the cargo bay was unprotected when they found themselves greeted by Zombies. The gunplay that exploded in the cargo hold would not go unnoticed by the crew of the zeppelin. Thankfully Grace and Baron Daedalus made quick work of the Zombies.

The doors above the Cargo hull opened and a lone figure entered and gazed below at the intruders. “You don’t take hints very well.” Nasrin barked.

“I am afraid not.” Baron Daedalus yelled back.

“I will have to kill you now.” Nasrin said as she unsheathed two scimitars from her back. The former companion of Baron Daedalus moved with inhuman speed and agility as she left from the railing above and landed on the cargo room floor.

Grace raised her pepper-boxes at the woman. Baron Daedalus singled for her to hold fire and he then turned to face Nasrin.

"What happened to you Nasrin?" Baron Daedalus questioned his old companion.

"As I lay dying in the volcano and not fully at peace with my sacrifice to kill Varney the Vampire, He called to me from his perilous position as the lava rose to claim him slowly." Nasrin paused as if collecting her memories.

"He, the very creature I sought to destroy out of loyalty to you, offered me the one thing you never did...Mira Jann"

"Eternal life," Baron Daedalus concluded, while ignoring the affectionate term from Nasrin.

"Correct...Do you think I liked the fact that my body was growing old and you were remaining ever youthful. An old solider is a dead one." Nasrin added.

Moments of silence passed between the estranged pair.

"So, this is my replacement, the notorious Grace Flynn, the Crimson Scarver. It would appear that you have chosen a lesser being." Nasrin spat.

"Nasrin, you do not need to help Varney with his plans, it is not too late for you to help us." Baron Daedalus pleaded.

"If I were still human, I might agree but now I am Vampire, and I am no longer bound to the weaknesses of humanity." Nasrin growled.

"I think this bloodsucker needs a bit of an arse-kicking." Grace shouted, she had grown quite tired of Nasrin, only having just met her.

Nasrin laughed and suddenly shoved Baron Daedalus aside like a ragdoll as she advanced toward Grace.

"I think it's high time you put steel were your mouth is!" Nasrin roared as she threw one of scimitars at Grace's feet. Grace needed no more invitation. She holstered her guns and kicked the sword up to her waiting hand.

"This is my dance; Baron Daedalus try not to kill Varney before I get there." Grace stated with a devilish smirk.

"You best hurry Mira Jann, once I kill this foolish woman. I will exterminate you next." Nasrin warned.

Baron Daedalus knew better than interfere and left Grace to face his past life, as he sought to save the future ones of others.

Grace initiated the first strike and it was parried by Nasrin. The women engaged in a complex dance of footwork and singing blades. Even without a Vampire's inhuman strength and agility Nasrin found Grace to be a worthy warrior.

"It would appear there is some truth to the tales about you. However, this where your story ends," Nasrin mocked as she lunged at

Grace, who spun out of the way like a deadly ballet dancer.

"You certainly do talk too much. Perhaps that is why Baron Daedalus left you to die in that volcano." Grace screamed.

Nasrin suddenly broke into a full-blown rage and unleashed a series of blows upon her foe. It took Grace every ounce of strength and agility to keep the Vampire at bay.

"You are going to die Flynn, and I will drink you like a vat of bloody wine." Nasrin laughed and rushed at her foe once more, her sword high.

The sound of a pepper-pot exploded as a slug ripped into Nasrin's top hat covered forehead. The Vampire staggered and looked bewildered.

"A soldier is taught how to fight with honor and defeat their enemy. I am a pirate; honor in battle is not my style." Grace spat and in one swift movement beheaded Nasrin before she could react.

Grace watched her enemy's head roll away as her body writhed on the floor. She cast the scimitar aside and looked for something that she could use to set the cargo area aflame. She knew once she lit the fire, she would have to quickly find Daedalus.

Grace was able to find a barrel full of whale oil and empty rum bottles in a storage closet. If there is one thing a pirate knows, it is how to make a fiery cocktail.

CHAPTER 24 - WINGS OF DEATH
REROUTE TO VENICE

Grace found Baron Daedalus and a flamboyantly dressed vampire locked in mortal combat upon the bridge. At last she had found the creature that had haunted her nightmares for so many years.

He looked younger than she remembered, and unexpectedly fetching. Varney suddenly gained the upper hand and threw Baron Daedalus against a nearby pilot's chair, knocking the wind out of him. Varney then noticed Grace.

"Well…what do we here? It would appear you have killed my dear Nasrin, no matter, I was growing tired of her anyway." Varney laughed. His ice blue eyes were full of ageless malice.

"You are the bastard that killed my father!" Grace screamed.

"Did I...It is so hard to keep track of those I devour and let me assure you, that you won't be remembered either." Varney leapt at Grace, who rolled out of the way emptying her pepper-boxes.

The Vampire realized he might be at a disadvantage and decided that he should live to terrorize another day. When he saw St. Mark's Square approaching through the blasted windows, he made his escape.

"This get together has been so very amusing, but I must take my leave. I am sorry, that I did not get to drink you dry. I am sure we shall meet again."

Baron Daedalus rushed to stop Grace from following Varney as he leapt out the ship's front window. Grace screamed in frustration as the Vampire escaped.

Grace broke free from Baron Daedalus, knocking him down. She ran to the window and saw Varney falling toward the earth below. She then turned to Baron Daedalus as he scrambled to his feet. A smile spread on her face as she leapt through the window after Varney.

Daedalus watched in horror as Grace opened her Icarus Glider and swooped at Varney. He saw Grace fumble with what appeared to be a small bottle and a familiar looking lightening gun. The bottle ignited and exploded as Grace caught fire. Now aflame she flew straight at Varney like a predatory bird, she slammed into him and spun wrapping him in her fiery wings.

Daedalus could hear Varney's screams as the flames licked his body and the mad laughter of Grace Flynn as she took revenge for her father.

The most dangerous woman alive and the Vampire fell to earth in a ball of flame. Baron Daedalus also leapt from the dirigible, when he realized it was also on fire as smoke came from below deck. His own Icarus Glider cranked open and he glided toward the nearby

Pendragon. The enemy dirigible now ablaze continued on its path to destruction out upon the open sea.

CHAPTER 25 - SAVING GRACE

ST. MARK'S SQUARE

Grace Flynn's broken body lay in the center of Mark's Square wrapped in the wire of her mechanical wings. A few feet away the charred remains of Varney smoldered in the setting sun.

Baron Daedalus slid down the rope dropped from the Pendragon as it hovered over the square below. He rushed to Grace and began to gently untangle the wings about her charred body. Tears were streaming from his eyes and he held Grace in comfort. The woman groaned in pain and too weak to speak.

Flammel soon joined his friend at Grace's side and he looked distraught as well. Baron Daedalus looked suddenly at Flammel.

"The stone, you must use the stone." Baron Daedalus pleaded.

“This is not your decision to make. Death might bring her peace now that she has exacted revenge.” Flammel advised his friend.

“I will not watch her die in this place; this is not how it shall end for Grace Flynn!” Baron Daedalus screamed. “You will use the stone to save her!”

“I understand your wish to save this young woman, but we are not Gods, old friend.”

“If this were Esmeralda would you stand on your moral high ground?” Baron Daedalus spat.

Flammel was at a loss for words. He then silently pulled a small chain from underneath his shirt. Upon it hung a silvery stone, to which he chanted strange spidery words. The stone flashed and he then placed it upon Grace’s charred forehead. The woman stopped writhing in pain and soon fell into a deep sleep.

“We must get her back to Paris; this shard will only ease her pain and will not stop death if it has come for her. Only the Philosopher’s Stone might save her now." Flammel informed Baron Daedalus.

"Then we best get going." Baron Daedalus commanded.

With the help of the Pendragon's crew Grace was gently taken aboard. Admiral Seagers promised to make for Paris with all the speed his vessel could muster. It did not take long for the Pendragon's engines to kick in high gear and force the vessel to sustain its maximum speed.

In the guest cabin Baron Daedalus sat vigilant at Grace's side as she slept. He refused both food and water as the flight to Paris was well underway. Flammel gave up trying to get his friend to rest and found a comfortable chair for himself and soon fell asleep.

CHAPTER 26 - GRACE'S DECISION

PARIS UNDERGROUND

Grace's conscious became aware of the sweet smell of roses and acrid chemicals. She took a deep breath and slowly creaked open her eyes. Her mind remembered the harrowing fall and the smell of her own skin aflame. Yet when she gazed upon her exposed skin it was perfect in every way. It was soft supple, free of charring and of all previous scars that once marked her flesh. She sat up and found herself upon a soft bed in a small room, which appeared to her as a laboratory of some sort. The room's small door groaned as it opened, and a familiar voice called out. "I see you are awake, are you decent?"

"Yes, Mister Flammel and do come in." Grace said excitedly and absently fixed her hair. Grace could only assume she was a complete mess, but she reasoned it did not matter. Being apparently unharmed and alive was far more appropriate.

Flammel's lab coat was covered in dry blood and he looked quite tired. His grey flecked hair was a complete mess and his blue eyes were extremely bloodshot. Despite all this his smile was warm and genuine. "You gave me quite a scare during your treatment. You were brought here in an awful mess. Yet he insisted that I fix you."

"He?" Grace asked though she already knew the answer.

"Baron Daedalus, my dear and I warned him the stone might not be enough to save you. You were so near death and in so much pain."

"You used the stone on me? Am I?"

"Immortal? No, I used the stone's healing power on you. Even with its power you were unconscious for many days. It has apparently done a great job in healing both new and old wounds. It also has given you back a few years of youth...I think something most valuable to a lady." Flammel suddenly blushed.

"Mister Flammel! You can't be serious. "Grace playfully hit him in the shoulder and blushed slightly as well.

"I assure you my observation was purely scientific in nature. Our age shows within the lines of our faces...particularly around the eyes. Your face now appears smooth and blemish free." Flammel's face darkened. "You should give up this folly with the Baron Daedalus and find a normal life. You have paid your debt to society I believe."

"A normal life is not the cards for me, Mister Flammel."

"You may call me Nicolas; there is no need for us to be formal among friends." Flammel stood and smiled. "The decision of future paths is yours; predetermination is for cowards. Something I know that Grace Flynn is most certainly not."

"Where is he?"

“I will let you him know that you are awake. He spent these past days by your side and only left at my stern command. He cares for you genuinely I think, perhaps you remind him of someone he once knew. Be kind to him Grace, but also be wary, his companionship is a most dangerous affair as you already know.”

Without another word Flammel left to fetch Baron Daedalus. Grace climbed out of bed and put on a nearby robe. She walked gingerly over to a nearby mirror and gazed within it. Despite her lack of attire, she was a vision of youthful beauty. Yet deep in her hazel eyes a fire burned one that could never be quenched even by a magical stone. Grace smiled and then her thoughts turned to her unknown future. She felt her heart flutter with a feeling of uncertainty. Before she could even begin to cope with the new emotions, the door opened once more.

"Nicolas says you have healed quite nicely." Baron Daedalus said while nervously dusting the sleeve of his pinstriped coat.

Grace turned, stormed over to the Baron Daedalus and before he could react, she slammed a fist into his face. Baron Daedalus stumbled backward. He straightened up and wiped a little blood from his now busted lip. A smile crept to his face, "Well I believe that brings us to even point."

Grace turned her back on the Daedalus, as tears began to peak from her eyes. She nonchalantly wiped them away hurriedly. A wave of mixed emotions burst into her chest and she could not reason why.

"Grace, I cannot truly exemplify my thankfulness to the magnitude of your bravery while in my service. I did however provide the details of your actions to the governments who require your imprisonment. They have unanimously agreed to eliminate all charges against you. You are a free woman and quite wealthy, considering what I have paid for your services." Baron Daedalus sighed and rubbed his jaw.

Grace turned to face Baron Daedalus. "You are the most big-headed man I have ever known. You revel in flaunting your own cleverness and seem to care nothing for the feelings of those around you. One might think you would relish no human company if you could make your inventions and books speak back to you." Grace could feel her face flush with anger as her unkempt hair fluttered upon her cheeks.

"Well it would appear you kept some of that fire in your blood from your most recent fall." Baron Daedalus halted any further quip when he saw Grace's fist clench once more.

"So, I am to understand that I am no longer under your employment."

"You are a free woman Grace Flynn, in the purest of definitions. While I found your work to be satisfactory during your employment, I know you may now wish to pursue other endeavors. The world can be most generous to a young, beautiful and wealthy woman.

I have made arrangements to put a quaint parcel of land, with a small cottage in your name and accounts drawn up for your new monetary holdings. I have also provided you with a new dossier outlining your clean background as a young heiress. Your father incidentally was made a ship captain, by the English government, who died off the coast of Borneo, to pirates, leaving all his assets to you. You know most people's identities are nothing more than a collection of records held by various government organizations. Since most we know tend forget us when we leave their sight."

"Does that mean I shall be forgotten when I leave your company?" Grace growled.

"I assure you Grace, one could never forget you. I have travelled this world for a very long span of time. I have never met anyone that would compare or overshadow you, Miss Flynn, in my eyes."

"So, what are you exactly saying Doctor?"

"I am clearly responding to your inquiries nothing more. You have fulfilled your debt to both government and your employer. You are free to seek your future through much less dangerous affairs."

"Why did you save me?"

"It was in your contract was it not?"

"I do not remember usage of the stone in the details of that agreement."

"You never cease to amaze me Grace; you are indeed a woman that could outwit most anyone if given the opportunity."

"What if I do not wish to leave? What if I wish to stay under your employment?"

"Impossible, your contract with me is fulfilled and I do not require anything else from you Miss Flynn. My life is dangerous to say the least and I do not wish to destroy this opportunity for you. You have lived a life of full of hardship and now a new prospect has appeared. I think you owe it to yourself to find serenity."

"None of this explains your saving me, and your vigil at my bedside. Nicolas was happy to divulge that fact."

"Grace what is it you seek for me to impart? To me you are still fragile despite your strengths. You were the rose growing in the desert and I did not wish to see you die from your thirst for revenge." Baron Daedalus paused and his eyes sparkled with a hidden emotion. "I asked the stone to be used because your light was not meant to be extinguished by me. You say that I am arrogant and do not wish the company of others. Here I must correct you. It is I who am not worthy of the company brought by people like you and Flammel." Grace moved to Baron Daedalus who raised a hand to stop her.

"Grace Flynn, a room has been prepared for you upstairs. Clothing and the required paper work for your new life await you. Please do not seek to change my position on this matter. You have done well take your reward and stray from things that may bring you harm once more." Baron Daedalus turned to leave.

It was then a realization formed in her mind, the events of her death unfolded in her memory and it reminded her of a story long ago. One she thought myth until the very legend found her.

"You did this because of Icarus." Grace said softly.

Baron Daedalus stopped in the doorway his hand gripped upon the door handle with apparent emotion.

"Know this Grace, fortunate is the soul that can find closure in a world that remains open with jaded perception. I did what anyone would have done, given the opportunity to save something of loveliness and to mend my own fractured soul if only in the smallest of ways. The act could be seen as purely selfish by most and perhaps it was just that."

"Well I am thankful then of your greedy heart."

Baron Daedalus closed the door and left Grace alone. The room seemed a bit colder now that she was once again alone. Her thoughts were a jumble of emotions and possibilities. She obviously had a great number of decisions to make, so she started by choosing to get dressed.

CHAPTER 27 - GRACE'S ANSWER

PARIS

The clothing provided by Baron Daedalus would have drawn envy from most young fashion-conscious maids. The navy-blue dress was tailored to Grace's lithe form perfectly. One could tell by the Doctor's impeccable attire he knew how to dress, but apparently, he could even make an ex-thief look fetching.

Grace had looked over the dossier upon her arrival and it all seemed in order. Everything she had ever wanted was now within her grasp. No longer would she have to rely on criminal activities to keep her fed and clothed. She had the means to live a life as a young heiress. The money Baron Daedalus had paid her was much more than she could have anticipated or even achieved on her own.

Yet despite this boon of good fortune Grace still felt empty inside, the fire that had burned within her for so many years, seemed to kindle and yearn to engulf her once more. But something was different now, burned out was the flame of revenge, it was replaced by a beacon of hope that would guide her to an unexpected prospect. A future that involved a man she had only just met, but under great peril had come to admire in a most surprising way. Grace knew what she had to do and left her quarters to embrace the change that had come to her.

Minutes later, she found Baron Daedalus in the library drinking a glass of wine and staring deep into the hearth as its amber flames licked the fresh wooden logs.

"Come to say goodbye?" Baron Daedalus said distantly.

"Yes, I have." Grace stated flatly.

"It is wise of you to seek another path and enjoy what life you have been presented. I am glad that I could help you on your way to happiness."

"Happiness is that what you call it?"

Baron Daedalus turned and looked at Grace. A look of bewilderment passed over his face. “Has madness taken you? You are free Grace Flynn, and all that comes with that title. You are wealthy, a goal that many strive for, and you have your youth something desired by many, myself included.”

“So now you are an expert on what makes Grace Flynn happy, how rash you are. Yes, I have had my revenge, but now I am free, and do you think I would give it up to be locked away in society and all that la-de-dah nonsense. Then you are a fool and really know nothing about me. I think you should update this dossier.” Grace shook the file prepared for her by Baron Daedalus in his face. “In fact, I think you should start over.” Grace barked and threw the file into the fireplace. Baron Daedalus made no move to stop her, but she did notice him smile slightly.

“So where do we go from here Miss Flynn?”

“First you are to hire me back and then you will take me to lunch, I am famished.”

“Grace, you do realize what you are giving up?”

“Baron Daedalus, I am well aware that your employment could ultimately bring about my demise. Yet I have never truly lived until meeting you. So, I am satisfied that my choice is the right one, for us both.”

“Now you assume to know my needs, Grace.” Baron Daedalus quipped.

“I know that few will keep your company willingly and besides someone has to keep you in line.” Grace retorted,

“Fine, Miss Grace Flynn, will you accept my offer of employment though it might ultimately see you to a most heinous end.” Baron Daedalus inquired.

“Yes, I do and who says you might not meet that heinous end?” Grace scoffed.

“Point taken; did you burn?” Baron Daedalus asked.

"You mean the banknotes and the property title? I may be hotheaded, but I am no fool. A girl needs a place for retirement once days of adventure are over." Grace informed her employer.

"Very good Grace now let's have lunch. I know a fabulous place owned by a vampire; they say the food is to die for." Baron Daedalus smiled in return.

He then offered his arm. Grace took it and together they left the library. Grace smiled as she listened to Baron Daedalus describe the menu and for the first time in her life, she was happy.

END

ATLAS OF DEATH

" A GRACE FLYNN TALE"

Grace entered the tavern and gazed at the patrons within the smoke-filled room. The menagerie of villains examined the newest arrival, some sneered, some moved into nearby shadows, others began to whisper to each other with wide eyes.

Grace smirked...She knew many in this place wanted to kill her and perhaps she would give them the opportunity. She felt no shame in welcoming their deadly advance and murdering them with little forethought. She had not survived this long, fearing strangers and their motives.

She silently scanned the room as she moved among the throng filled with brigands and questionable locals, all who felt the need to give her a death glare and nothing more, till one seadog, felt his territory was being invaded. The heavy smell of salt, ale, and tobacco proceeded the brute as he grabbed Grace's shoulder.

"Yur..kind is not welcome here...Sea Witch!" The man spat with drunken enthusiasm.

Grace stopped. Suddenly the flowing tendrils of her long red scarf, wrapped like angry constrictors upon the man's arm. The pirate spun on her heels, her signature pepperbox gun clicked to life and it rushed through the air to meet the man's flabby jowls.

The man winced as the strange scarf tightened on his arm, beads of sweat burst upon his forehead. A hush fell over the tavern as all eyes watched Grace and her newfound enemy locked in a deadly dance.

"I don't remember askin' your permission, perhaps you would like to trade some lead for me entrance fee?" Grace smiled wickedly.

The man quickly realized that in his attempt to pick out prey, he had found a deadly predator. "My apologies, I did not recognize you in this low light, Captain Flynn."

Grace sneered at the man and pushed her gun deeper into the flesh of his fat neck. "I see...well let's help you to not forget."

The strike came quickly as Grace's gun smashed into the man's nose; blood erupted as a resounding crack echoed within the tavern. The sailor moaned in pain and gripped his nose when Grace's scarf released its hold upon his arm. The wounded man scurried away like a defeated bully and the tavern
suddenly sprung back to life as if nothing had ever occurred.

Grace looked about the room, to see if any other dance partners felt the need to join her. None sought to approach her, and Grace walked around the nearby bar and headed to a more secluded room located at the back of the building. The men here were far more dangerous and important than the ruffians Grace had encountered upon her entrance. Many of the pirate captains eyed Grace but did not engage her, a few their guards however reached for various weapons as she passed them by.

"Well, Luv...you certainly know how to make a dramatic entrance." A voice remarked ahead of Grace. She gritted her teeth upon hearing the endearing term, that she despised most deeply. She located the origin of the voice. A tall lean man waved her over with his many-ringed hand.

Grace stormed over and pointed a finger at the man. "Must I tell you repeatedly not to call me that?" Grace barked.

The man's bearded face broke into a smile, it was obviously a fake one.

"Grace...I assure you, after your recent display of congeniality. I have no intentions of angering you." The man motioned to a table upon which sat two tankards brimming with ale.

"Shut yer saucebox...Nereus and let's have this get-together over with." Grace growled and sat at the table, she reached for the ale and took a healthy swig. She wiped the froth off her face with the sleeve of her coat.

The man named Nereus sat opposite of his guest and took a sip of his ale as well. He then drummed his long fingers upon the wooden table, eyeing Grace intently. Grace looked in return and raised her chin in mock defiance.

"Grace...I have a need, to disappear upon the waves for a bit." Nereus stated flatly.

"Made new friends have we?" Grace paused and let her comment sink in. "Why should I help you avoid the wrath of your mistakes?" Grace questioned her host.

"Always so direct, a good quality I assure you. However, I have something that you will find most interesting." Nereus offered cryptically.

Grace laughed suddenly. "Are you going to offer me a map to some buried treasure for my help?"

Nereus smiled awkwardly. "No certainly not. I have something far more valuable." He then leaned in and whispered low, "I have in my possession the Atlas of Death."

Grace went silent and her mocking smile faded.

Silence hung in the air between them, Nereus could tell Grace was absorbing his last statement and calculating a response.

"Before you ask, I had the handwriting confirmed by his own brother, who is currently enjoying an extended stay, in one of Her Majesty's more eloquent prisons, in the heart of England," Nereus added.

"Let me see it," Grace demanded.

"Really Luv, do you think I would bring it here among such refined," Nereus remarked as he moved his head to indicate the company about them. "I have this as proof." Nereus reached in his coat and pulled out a handkerchief wrapped around a small object.

He then slid the parcel across the table to Grace.

Grace moved her empty tankard aside and reached quickly for the object. She took it in her hands and proceed to carefully open the cloth. Inside, she found a fresh red wax impression, it was still slightly warm. She instantly recognized the symbol from a flag she had seen once...long ago. Thankfully its ship and her crew were busy destroying a British warship. Allowing Grace to quickly leave the area without drawing attention to her own vessel. But the mere sighting of the legendary vessel and its memory brought a cold chill presently to her spine.

"How did you come upon this?" Grace said crushing the wax quickly and wrapping it once more in the handkerchief.

"That is a story for another time," Nereus replied vaguely.

Grace leaned back in her chair. "This is a dangerous gambit, one that could get us both killed."

"When has that ever stopped either of us before?" Nereus asked with a grin.

"Is it true?" Grace questioned.

"That it contains the locations to his vast spoils?" Nereus inquired and he nodded silently.

"He will hunt you if he knows you possess it," Grace remarked.

"Ahh...but dead men don't tell tales," Nereus informed.

"I want two-thirds of the take," Grace demanded.

"Really Luv, the best I can offer is half." Nereus bartered.

"Two-thirds or you can try your luck with any of the honest men for hire in this place." Grace waved her hands about.

"Fine...I accept your terms." Nereus said through his teeth.

Grace stood and straightened her coat. She nodded at Nereus and turned to leave. "We sail at dawn. You best bring your book with you next time."

"I shall Flynn...I shall." Nereus said putting on his plumed cavalier hat and standing to leave as well.

Grace turned one last time and eyed Nereus from under her tricorn. Her long ruddy scarf's tendrils fluttered unnaturally behind her. Nereus knew that Grace's red adornment was not an ordinary cloth. It was a Bloodsilk, that had once belonged to a Redcap, a malevolent creature that Grace had somehow killed long ago. Grace was already a formidable opponent to any scallywag, but her supernatural artifact made her extremely dangerous. It was the source of her power and the reason for her moniker, The Crimson Scarver.

"One day that ruddy thing will consume you whole," Nereus warned.

"Don't be late you fop," Grace spat mockingly and left.

PART II

"Welcome back...Captain, how is the dandy today?" A female voice asked playfully. Grace looked up as she walked the plank up to her ship the Lokothea. A tall and pale woman with a flaming, red mane of hair, grinned displaying fang-like canine teeth.

Grace chuckled in response. "None worse for the wear, Brona, I suppose. Where is Seaton?"

"He is out stockin' up on supplies. hopefully scotch as well." Brona informed.

Grace looked about her ship and noticed most of the crew were, not present. Her visage turned dark. "Gather the crew and I would advise that you feed quietly, you may need your strength."

"Aye...So Nereus had made friends once agin'," Brona assumed.

"Are we stocked on powder and lead?" Grace asked.

"Now...I wouldn' be a good highlander if I didn' keep my devil's toys at hand. So many British playmates to share 'em with." Brona replied playfully.

"Good...If you see Seaton tell him, we sail at dawn. You best get movin', eat and find my crew." Grace commanded.

"Aye...consider it dun' Captain," Brona said as she grabbed her nearby claymore and left the ship.

PART III

Grace set her pepperbox gun down on her table within her Captain's cabin. She momentarily gazed at a map upon the table. It depicted the known seas and lands within them. She silently wondered where the treasures of Captain Death lay hidden. She knew that working with Nereus Neptune, was like playing a game of noddy, where the cards don't add up. She could possibly lose and Nereus might very well gain for it.

Grace knew that Captain Death was dangerous and many on the seas feared his wrath in any form. Her own gunner, Bloody Brona, knew all too well, what crossing this particular villain meant. Brona's entire clan had paid for robbing Captain Death's ship when it had docked off the Scottish coast. Brona had survived but not without the bearing the curse of her clan. Grace could not imagine the horrors the

Scottish maiden had seen before the darkness had consumed her.

A heavy knock on her cabin door pulled her from sailing among her inner thoughts. "Enter," was Grace's reply.

A large Nubian man entered, placed a full bottle of mead on Grace's table. He smiled then stood straight and crossed his thick muscled arms. Grace grabbed the mead, pulled its cork and took a whiff of the liquid contents held within. She then sealed the jug and placed it back on the table.

"I trust you have gotten all we need, without bleeding my coffers." Grace teased.

"That I have Captain...I hear that we are going to have Master Neptune aboard, should I prepare the brig?" Seaton grinned at his own humor.

"Not yet at least. However, make sure you have nothing valuable in your quarters since he will be bunking with ya." Grace shot back.

"Yes...I figured as much, we don't need Brona feeding on him," Seaton paused. "Captain, may I ask what he has in mind?"

"You may...The answer is simple; we are hunting treasure that might get us killed all the same." Grace said plainly.

"It is of my knowledge, that gaining treasure always comes with death as an alternative prize." Seaton reasoned.

"Yes...Death is the gambit and holder on this matter."

"If I am understanding you correctly, then we are flirting with the devil himself. How does Nereus plan to rob this demon?"

"The Atlas," Grace answered. "Does this course worry you...Seaton?"

"As long... as your hands guide the wheel of the Lokothea, I worry for nothing. I only hope this man knows what he is doing. For his sake." Seaton grinned and this caused Grace to smirk in return.

"Speak none of this to the crew, tell them only we are looking for trade vessels, and Nereus has the logs of their routes," Grace stated firmly.

Seaton nodded. "Did you approve of the mead?"

"It's a fine smelling brew," Grace replied.

"I was told that it was made
in Caerdydd. I thought it might suit you." Seaton noted.

"Thank you, Seaton, that will be all...old friend." Grace then waved him off with a flip of her hand.

Seaton bowed slightly and left his Captain to plan for the events that Nereus Neptune would no doubt bring to the decks of her beloved ship.

PART IV

"She has agreed to take the task," Nereus replied to his host. The pirate could not help but admire the opulence and array of artifacts contained within the room he now sat.

"Well done, it is my hope that Grace will be up to the task at hand." the well-dressed man replied.

"Captain Death is a very wicked enemy to make," Nereus remarked.

"Yes...but, Grace Flynn is the most dangerous woman alive. She has outwitted or killed some of the most diabolical and intelligent men both upon the land and among the waves. She is the only chance; the Veiled Society has of destroying this particular villain."

"Perhaps...She will become more dangerous than the monster you seek to unleash her upon. Also, there is the possibility, that you might very well get her killed." Nereus warned.

"I am quite sure that Grace Flynn will become a force to be reckoned with. Know that I have foreseen this and prepared for the inevitability that she must be dealt with." Nereus' host stated coldly.

"Well, I shall keep you informed of our progress when I can and I will see to it that she finds the sword as well," Nereus remarked then stood and put on his caviler hat. "Baron Metion are you sure there is no other way to destroy Captain Death?"

Baron Metion looked at Nereus and straightened his pinstriped vest absently. "I am sure that this matter must be dealt with and Grace Flynn is the weapon of my own choice." Nereus nodded in return and then left the room. As the pirate took his leave of Baron Metion's offices and made way to the inn that he had selected for the evening, he could not help but feel a sour pit growing in his stomach.

He had known Grace for many years, and he had a fondness for her, akin to a bond, he once held for another woman that he had lost tragically so long ago...his sister, Nerea. The pirate knew he was betraying Grace by working with Baron Metion and he was assuredly placing her in grave danger.

Yet, Captain Death was a matter of grave concern, and it was only a matter of time before the Crown, became involved. Nereus' recent meeting with the Queen had not gone well and Her Majesty was insistent that if Baron Metion did not handle the matter, England would.

Baron Metion, however, had seemed unmoved by the Queen's ultimatum. The Baron simply told Nereus to inform the Queen, the Her Majesty's intervention would only complicate the issue. If this did not appease Her Majesty, then Baron Metion would seek council with the Crown, himself. The life of a pirate and double-agent was getting complicated and Nereus needed a drink to clear his head, and perhaps some company to share his bed before he headed to sea.

PART V

The crew of the Lokothea had returned with haste and were busy prepping the ship for its departure. Grace watched Seaton bark his orders to the men and could hear Brona yelling to her gunners below as they stacked cannons in preparation for battle if it arose.

The wind caused the Lokothea's red sails to flutter as the crew checked them for any areas that needed repair. Grace eyed the Welsh flag that whipped from her main mast. She suddenly longed to raise her Jolly Roger and smell the salty air mixed with the sting of gunpowder smoke. To hear the roar of battle and the clash of steel. The sun was only a few hours away and the sea called to Grace like a forgotten lover. Grace smiled softly, whatever loomed ahead of her, mattered not, as she turned to go below deck her Bloodsilk's tendrils dance rhythmically, perhaps it too sensed the adventure that was to come.

PART V.I

"There is an island a few leagues from our present position. We must stop there to have the wards on the atlas removed. We cannot discern the true locations unless this is done." Nereus told Grace as he rand his finger across the map on her table to a small island no more than a dot in its representation.

"That is the Isle of the Witch," Seaton noted.

"Full disclosure has never been your best quality...Nereus," Grace Spat.

"I assure you Grace it was for the best. I thought to tell you to sail to a witch's island might make you less prone to let me aboard." Nereus stated in a sarcastic tone.

"I think it might be the best heave you overboard," Grace replied and nodded to Seaton who moved toward Nereus.

"My apologies...Grace, no more withheld information." Nereus quickly promised. To

which Grace nodded once more and Seaton, then took his leave from Grace's cabin.
Grace waited for her cabin to close and then let loose on Nereus. "Have you lost all your wits in that hat of yours?" Grace snapped and the scowled. "Seafaring men are
superstitious enough, and then you want to go sailing to an island with a witch like you are on holiday."

"Grace if we do not break the hexes upon this book, it will lead us straight back to Captain Death." Nereus Warned.

"What do you mean...speak plainly," Grace demanded.

"It is said the book will cause its holder, to bring it back to its master. Right now, I keep the book locked in a cold iron box, to confine its magic. Yet I am unsure how long or if the cold iron will restrain the spells upon it. The Witch Kirabo is well versed in the lore of hexes, truth be told, they may very well be her own handiwork."

"So your plan is to go to the witch who created the hexes for the man who would kill us for stealing his Atlas." Grace surmised.

"Put like that, it certainly seems a bit flawed. Yet, Kirabo holds not loyalties and wealth is of little use to her. I have a feeling suitable payment for her services can be arranged." Nereus informed his host.

"Well if its sacrifice she needs, I'll see that you volunteer. I will set course, best not mention our destination to anyone else on my crew." Grace advised and the ushered Nereus out of her cabin.

PART VII

The man screamed terribly as the skin was flayed from his body. It had taken some time to get the answers, but Captain Death now had a name...Nereus Neptune. The
Captain gazed at his first mate who stood with the cat-o-nine tails in his grip. The brute huffed with and unnatural rage and desire to tear the prisoner asunder.

"I no longer have a need for that blood-bag." Captain Death informed his crewman.

As he turned to leave the brig of his ship, he heard his first mate tear into the flesh of the prisoner and feed upon him. Captain Death grinned with delight as he heard the snap of the prisoner's neck.

PART VIII

Grace stepped upon the shoreline of the small island. She gazed about and noticed the dense forest the covered most of the small island. Grace had often played as a child in the dark forests of the Welsh coast, but this particular wood seemed much more menacing.

"Unfortunately, the abode of this woman is deep in that bramble and branch." Nereus indicated as he walked up to Grace's side.

"Dis' quest gets more cumbersome by the minute," Brona noted as she and Seaton pulled the dingy ashore.

"I have a written account of where the hovel lies within but no map," Nereus informed.

"Have your wits about you, lead on Nereus." Grace commended as she unholstered her pepperbox gun.

The small band of pirates strode into the wood cautiously, all the time aware of their surroundings. No sounds could be heard but their own footfalls. The forest seemed to be devoid of all life and an unease began to fall upon the small party.

"How much further to this conjurer's lair?" Seaton asked.

"The notes indicate she located near the island's center," Nereus responded.

"Of course, she would be deep in the dark wood," Grace smirked.

The group continued their progression through the dense trees when suddenly their path led to a great opening. The clearing looked as if an immense fire had burned deep within the woods. The petrified remains of great trees lay scattered about and the ground was charred and black. As Grace and her crew strode out into the clearing, the sound of rubble moving and the strange sound of joints popping echoed all about. The group of pirates was suddenly surrounded by the remains of those how had tread to this place before them.

Skeletons of all shapes and adornment came to life and moved toward them like a small army.

"Tis' that in your notes fop?" Brona barked, drawing her claymore.

"I am afraid not, any chance you can speak to fellow dead folk and have them stand down?" Nereus asked in return.

Grace ignored the banter and fired upon an approaching skeleton its skull exploded and its bones fell to earth to move no more. The crew needed no further example and began to smash, lop off, or shoot every skull that got too close. The battle was fast and soon not a single skeletal corpse moved.

"Is there anything in your scant notes that we should be aware of before we continue?" Grace stated as she suddenly fired on a skeleton that appeared from the nearby tree line. The undead creature fell lifelessly as it skull left its body.

"I am afraid not, but we should be nearing her dwelling soon," Nereus noted.

PART IX

The boiling cauldron showed the invaders had survived the skeletal trap and would soon be at her doorstep. Kirabo laughed to herself and smiled revealing her filed and pointed teeth. A crow squawked behind her and the witch turned to face it.

"You are right Cynbel, I should prepare for our guests. I look dreadful." Kirabo cackled and stretched her ancient body. Using her cane, she moved to a trapdoor in the floor of her shelter. She waved her hand the door flung open revealing a stone staircase below The Witch entered the opening and muttered a spidery word, suddenly a glowing ball of flame appeared and hovered above her right shoulder, lighting her way. The room below was filled with jars of various things, some alive while others were quite dead. The sound of rattling chains sounded from a corner to the left, ahead of the Witch.

"Hello dear...I only need a bit of flesh and blood." Kirabo mused to her permanent guest.

The muffled screams of her victim echoed in the small cellar, as the Witch grabbed a nearby knife. She cackled softly as she closed in on the young man chained to the wall, the stumps of his legs moving frantically in a vain attempt to get away.

PART X

Captain Death gazed upon the sea, from the deck of his ship, The Terrible, as his mind raced for answers. He knew that his Atlas had been stolen, but by whom was still a mystery. He knew that his crew was loyal at least his officers. The others would have to be tortured until the maggot was found.

His first mate, a vampire named Lt. Devil walked up and saluted him. "We have found the man." He stated flatly.

"Good and what did we discover before he is to be consumed?" Captain Death asked while his face broke into a grin.

"The man named Nereus Neptune is our target, he is also a known ally of Grace Flynn." Lt. Devil revealed.

"Grace Flynn, the Crimson Scarver...How delightful." Captain Death paused, "We must not keep the Lokothea waiting, we shall make its deck run with the red it displays in her sails." Captain Death promised.

"Yes Sir, I shall send crows and discover her whereabouts." Lt. Devil then left to perform his duties.

Captain Death leaned on the nearby ship's rail, his hands gripped the wooden structure violently, the wood cracked in response. "Your days of slinking out of my reach are drawing to a close Flynn, now that you have Neptune aboard and my Atlas."

The Terrible's surgeon, Ghost stepped out on the deck dragging a brutally beat man. He walked unhindered with his human baggage and proceeded to load the man into a large guillotine mounted on the back of the ship. A great trough opened from the front of the execution device.

"Care for a drink, my Captain?" Ghost asked as he lowered the neck brace upon his victim.

Captain Death walked to the trough, reached in and pulled out a golden jewel-encrusted goblet, stained with dry blood.

"I am thirsty, and we should not let this maggot's blood go to waste." Captain Death held up his cup. "Traitors are best served quickly to the lips of Death."

The traitorous crewman did little to squirm and perhaps welcomed his demise rather than face more abuse. The hungry guillotine whooshed as it rushed to severe the man's neck. A resounding thump of the blade and tear of flesh along with the cut of bone echoed. The man's head plopped into the trough along with a fresh rush of blood.

Ghost quickly opened the guillotine and grabbed the man's corpse, he then hung it on a hook dangling nearby to allow all the victim's blood to drain into the trough.

Captain Death dipped his goblet into the pool of blood. He filled his cup and drank with satisfaction as if he was partaking in freshly brewed mead.

"A bit bitter but refreshing none the less." Captain Death said and took another glass. "I relish the day to drink...Grace Flynn."

TO BE CONTINUED IN:
GRACE FLYNN - TIAMAT

AUTHOR BIO

Philip Cathalson is the pen name for (Philip McCall II), CEO & President of Cathal Entertainment, a multimedia production company located in South Florida.

Cathalson is the creator of the Grace Flynn Chronicles and the RPG narrative game Might & Mystic.

Along with his growing collection of personal intellectual properties, Cathalson also leads the further development of several existing properties for other organizations, through fiction lines published exclusively by Cathal Entertainment.

SUMMER 2019

BOOK II: GRACE FLYNN CHRONICLES
FALL 2019

REALMS
OF PARLOUS
THE THIEF OF THORNS
THE JINNFLOWER WARS : BOOK ONE
CATHALSON

FALL 2019

AVAILABLE AT ALL BOOKSELLERS

SUMMER 2019

#1
PENNY and Dime
WRITTEN BY: CATHALSON

TALES

VOLUME ONE

COMING
FALL 2019

www.ingramcontent.com/pod-product-compliance
Lightning Source LLC
Chambersburg PA
CBHW070629310726
48982CB00001B/226